HER FINAL WORD

A JACK RYDER NOVEL

WILLOW ROSE

BOOKS BY THE AUTHOR

HARRY HUNTER MYSTERY SERIES

- All The Good Girls
- Run Girl Run
- No Other Way
- Never Walk Alone

MARY MILLS MYSTERY SERIES

- What Hurts the Most
- You Can Run
- You Can't Hide
- Careful Little Eyes

EVA RAE THOMAS MYSTERY SERIES

- Don't Lie to me
- What you did
- Never Ever
- Say You Love me
- Let Me Go
- It's Not Over
- Not Dead yet

EMMA FROST SERIES

- Itsy Bitsy Spider
- Miss Dolly had a Dolly
- Run, Run as Fast as You Can
- Cross Your Heart and Hope to Die
- Peek-a-Boo I See You
- Tweedledum and Tweedledee

- Easy as One, Two, Three
- There's No Place like Home
- Slenderman
- Where the Wild Roses Grow
- Waltzing Mathilda
- Drip Drop Dead
- Black Frost

JACK RYDER SERIES

- Hit the Road Jack
- Slip out the Back Jack
- The House that Jack Built
- Black Jack
- Girl Next Door
- Her Final Word
- Don't Tell

REBEKKA FRANCK SERIES

- One, Two...He is Coming for You
- Three, Four...Better Lock Your Door
- Five, Six...Grab your Crucifix
- Seven, Eight...Gonna Stay up Late
- Nine, Ten...Never Sleep Again
- Eleven, Twelve...Dig and Delve
- Thirteen, Fourteen...Little Boy Unseen
- Better Not Cry
- Ten Little Girls
- It Ends Here

MYSTERY/THRILLER/HORROR NOVELS

- Sorry Can't Save You
- In One Fell Swoop
- Umbrella Man

- Blackbird Fly
- To Hell in a Handbasket
- Edwina

HORROR SHORT-STORIES

- Mommy Dearest
- The Bird
- Better watch out
- Eenie, Meenie
- Rock-a-Bye Baby
- Nibble, Nibble, Crunch
- Humpty Dumpty
- Chain Letter

PARANORMAL SUSPENSE/ROMANCE NOVELS

- In Cold Blood
- The Surge
- Girl Divided

THE VAMPIRES OF SHADOW HILLS SERIES

- Flesh and Blood
- Blood and Fire
- Fire and Beauty
- Beauty and Beasts
- Beasts and Magic
- Magic and Witchcraft
- Witchcraft and War
- War and Order
- Order and Chaos
- Chaos and Courage

THE AFTERLIFE SERIES

- Beyond
- Serenity
- Endurance
- Courageous

THE WOLFBOY CHRONICLES

- A Gypsy Song
- I am WOLF

DAUGHTERS OF THE JAGUAR

- Savage
- Broken

PROLOGUE

LYFORD CAY, THE BAHAMAS

MARCH 2018

THE DARK OCEAN RAGED AGAINST THE SIDES OF THE BOAT. THEY were going fast through the choppy waters, speeding through the night, laughing and holding hands. Ella Maria Chauncey and Henry Sakislov were standing in the front where splashes of water hit their faces. Their friends, Claire and Sebastian, were sitting in the back, making out on top of empty champagne bottles. Ella urged Henry to go even faster, and the boat almost flew across the waves, bumping across them, while she laughed wildly.

"Faster still," she said. "Faster."

Henry shook his head. "You're wild; do you know that?"

She laughed, and he pushed the boat up to its top speed.

Behind them, in the far distance, she could see the lights from Lyford Cay dancing, and she wished they could just keep going, just continue till they reached Cuba or maybe the Keys. Maybe they could go even further than that. Just disappear, get out of here. Start a new life somewhere else. She was fed up with her life and their gated community. Ella wanted to see the world.

"We should be getting back now," Henry said and slowed down. "Before our parents send out the Coast Guard to find us."

"No," Ella said and stared into the darkness ahead, where

promises of different countries and exotic cultures called to her. "Not yet."

Henry looked at his watch. "It's almost midnight. Aren't you scared that they'll find out that you've snuck out? That you've gone boating in the middle of the night?"

Ella sighed and looked into Henry's eyes. He was such a kid. He didn't know anything, did he? Not about her life, he didn't. She had never told him anything. But, for once, he was actually right about one thing. It was a cliché to say that your parents would kill you if they found out you had done something they didn't approve of, but in her case, she did fear for her life when she got back home, even more than the sharks in the ocean in front of her.

"Ella?"

She shook her head. "Sorry. I drifted off for just a second."

"Are we going back or what?" Claire asked and looked at her 2.4 million-dollar Rolex that her dad had given her for her sweet sixteen. "I have to get back."

"My dad is hosting a party, so I can stay out all night if I like," Sebastian said. "He'll never notice that I'm gone."

Henry scoffed. "Your dad never notices if you're gone."

Sebastian chuckled and emptied the last bottle of champagne. "Truth, dear friend."

"Claire is right," Henry said. "It's getting late. We really should be heading back."

He turned the boat while Ella exhaled, dissatisfied. She hated having to go back and could have gone on forever, the wind blowing in her face, continuing into oblivion where no one could hurt her.

Ever.

LYFORD CAY, THE BAHAMAS

MARCH 2018

THEY DOCKED THE BOAT BEHIND HENRY'S DAD'S HOUSE AND WENT back on shore. Ella looked at the many lights coming from the mansion where he lived. It was more than a hundred and fifty thousand square feet and housed almost a small city of in-house help, trying to maintain the big property. Ella herself had grown up on a similar property—even though it was smaller—with almost as many people working for her, so it wasn't that part that bothered her family.

It was Henry's dad. Henry's father was a hard-partying retail tycoon. He was pompous and didn't belong in Lyford Cay with his long grey hair and Hugh Hefner-lifestyle. And, worst of all, he once tried to buy their property, offering them way below what it was worth. That didn't go over well. To Ella, it was just an offer, but the Chaunceys saw it as a threat. Everything about the Sakislovs was an abomination, according to the Chaunceys. The Sakislovs belonged to the newly rich. And they were destroying everything in the small quiet gated community that had, up until some years ago, only been for the few. Now, they had invaded it and were bound to destroy everything it stood for. Henry's dad, Sergei, in the front of the line with his lifestyle of partying and women, bringing in the worlds of fashion, celebrities, and shiny new money. He was going to turn this place into Hollywood or even worse, West Palm Beach, swarming their once-so-secluded paradise with Russian oligarchs, software-company-owners-turned-millionaires-overnight, yoga bloggers, and You-Tube celebrities. It was a concern shared with a lot of other long-term inhabitants of the exclusive neighborhood.

To Ella, it seemed ridiculous. They all lived in mansions that were worth hundreds of millions of dollars—even though Ella's family's estate was less than half the size of Henry's dad's and therefore only worth about half the money, not to mention a lot less overwhelmingly decorated. They all had their houses filled with imported household help, maids, and garden people.

What did it even matter?

Claire and Ella hugged goodbye, and Ella watched her best friend help her boyfriend across the lawn to their golf cart they had parked there when they arrived. Sebastian insisted he wasn't too wasted to drive and took the wheel. Ella chuckled as she watched him zigzag across the lawn, scaring a flock of the three-hundred peacocks, parrots, and cockatoos that Henry's dad had free-ranging on his property.

Henry grabbed Ella's hand and kissed the top of it.

"I had a wonderful time," she said. "I wish we could do this every night."

Henry sighed and they walked toward the house, him holding his arm over her shoulder.

"Me too," he said.

There was something in the way he said it that had her worried. It had been in his eyes all night long. A sadness that she couldn't really figure out. Was something wrong between them? Was he breaking up with her? Did he know what she had done?

They walked inside and through one of the dining rooms, where Henry's dad had his fifty-foot dining table that could drop down into the floor and become a disco dance floor, once dinner, and bird droppings, were cleared. Ella chuckled when thinking about all the many times she had been at the house when younger for karaoke nights, where a flock of the young women he sometimes had staying with him danced while Henry's dad sang *I Did it My Way*.

She missed those times when their families didn't quarrel. When she could hang out with Henry anytime she wanted.

Henry kissed her forehead as they walked through the thirty-thousand-square-foot grand hall with its huge glass ceilings that Henry had once told Ella weighed a hundred thousand pounds.

Why the forehead and not my lips?

He walked her to the front door and closed it behind him. In the distance, they could hear the party Henry's dad was hosting by the pool at one of the guesthouses. It was far enough away for anyone not to be able to see Ella and Henry together.

Henry leaned over and finally kissed her properly. He smelled of champagne and ocean.

"You could stay," he said. "Sneak out in the morning?"

"That's probably not a good idea," she said.

"Why not?" he said, disappointed once again. He seemed aggressive in his way of talking to her, more than usual when she refused him.

They had been dating for a year now, and Ella hadn't been giving him what he wanted. She held it back, simply because she knew that was what you needed to do with a guy like Henry. He was used to girls throwing themselves at him and giving him everything, so he grew tired of them quickly. Keeping him chasing you was the only way to maintain his interest. But it left him frustrated every time.

"Come on," he said and kissed her again.

She pushed him away. "Not now, Henry."

He kissed her once more, holding her face between his hands so she couldn't move away.

"You're drunk," she said.

"So what?" he asked. "Since when does that stop you? Since when does anything hold you back from sleeping with anyone?"

"What are you talking about?" she said and pushed him away.

Henry always got worse when he was drunk. More demanding

and entitled. This was the point when she needed to leave. She smiled, then stood on her tiptoes.

"You know I don't do drunks," she said and kissed his soft lips, then walked off, holding her sandals in her hand. Her swimsuit underneath her dress was still wet and had soaked the dress, keeping her nice and cool in the warm night.

"Ah, come on," he said, "You can't just leave me hanging like this?"

But she didn't give him more. Knowing she had to get away from him quickly, she waved casually.

"You sure I shouldn't walk you home at least?" he yelled after her, his voice quivering with the same sadness she had seen in his eyes.

She turned, and her dress swirled around as she walked backward, facing him.

"I'll be fine. Besides, you don't want anyone to see us together, do you?"

"I don't care," he said.

"I do."

"Are you sure?" he asked. "I could walk you halfway?"

"I'll be fine," she said.

"You sure?" he said, his eyes glaring at her hungrily.

She nodded. "Yes. It's a gated community, remember? What could possibly happen?"

LYFORD CAY, THE BAHAMAS

MARCH 2018

SHE FELT LIGHTHEADED FROM THE CHAMPAGNE STILL IN HER VEINS, but remotely happy. Ella felt hopeful at this moment in her life for the first time in months. Turning sixteen made her even closer to that magical eighteen that she had longed for her entire life. The year when she would finally be able to leave, to decide for herself what to do, and do whatever she wanted.

She was supposed to go to Harvard. She knew it was expected, but Ella had other plans. There was an entire world out there waiting just for her and, like the European kids she often met at Jaw's Beach, she wanted to travel. She wanted to get away. And with the way things were, she probably would never return to what she often referred to as her prison because of the gates and the guards.

For most people, it was a dream to grow up in the Bahamas, but not for Ella. She dreamt of different places. She dreamt of New York and Paris. Her family owned condos in both places, so she wanted to stay in one of those, maybe go to an acting school, become an actress. She just hadn't quite figured out how to ask for it yet, and she kept postponing it, probably because she knew how her family felt about acting and Hollywood. It was going to kill them. Ella had always been the good girl, the one who did everything she was supposed to and never complained. It was going to come as a shock to everyone, especially to Henry. She wasn't sure if she loved him; for Ella, love had always been strange, and she wasn't sure she knew exactly how real love felt. But she liked him. She had fun with him.

For now.

Ella hummed as she walked down the road. In the distance, she could still hear the ocean as the waves crashed onto the shore and she enjoyed the smell of it. That was one thing she was going to miss once she left. The ocean. The turquoise blue ocean and snorkeling at the reefs. She had done that since she was just a young child and would definitely miss that part.

The rest? Not so much.

She walked in the grass on the side of the road, letting her toes sink into the thick grass and chuckled when it tickled her. She and Henry were neighbors, but since both properties were so big, there was a long way for her to walk home. Henry's estate went all the way to the end of the island. Sakislov Pointe it was called now. His dad had convinced the local government to rename it, much to most of the inhabitants at Lyford Cay's regret. Ella chuckled when thinking about all the trouble that man had caused in the neighborhood. It had been quite entertaining to watch while growing up along with his son. Ella didn't understand what the fuss was about. She liked Mr. Sakislov. He had always been very nice to her.

Ella felt a sudden shiver and sped up. She passed the main entrance to Henry's estate—what was often referred to at her household as The Russian Invasion. It had pompous marble statues outside, almost monuments that were staring down at her, making her uncomfortable. It was like they were scolding her for being out so late.

Ella hurried. It wasn't so far anymore. She had never been out this late in their neighborhood, and what usually made her feel safe and almost smothered, now gave her an uneasy feeling. The huge statues suddenly looked like monuments on graves.

Ella took a deep breath and sped up more. A flock of black vultures took off from a treetop and startled her. She was running now. Running to get home faster, hurrying through the darkness, jumping from streetlight to streetlight.

Almost there, Ella, she reassured herself. *Just a little further down the road.*

An iguana stared at her while sitting on a rock, its eyes flickering back and forth on the side of its head. Ella ran past it, her heart pounding in her chest. There was a smell of rain in the air, and she worried a storm might be coming.

Ahead of her in the road, she spotted a shadow. Ella stopped running. The figure stood still, glaring at her. It suddenly took off and rushed toward her. Ella gasped and stood like she was frozen at first, until she realized this person was coming after her.

By then, it was too late.

Ella turned around and ran while the perpetrator's shoes were clapping loudly on the asphalt behind her, coming closer and closer.

PART I

1

Nassau, Bahamas, October 2018

"I can't find anyone by that name anywhere. I am sorry."

The woman behind the old computer didn't look up at me as she said the words. I stared at her, doubting she had even tried. She had barely touched the keyboard in front of her.

"Please," I said and pointed at Emily sitting beside me. "I'm trying to find her family. I've tried online; I've been to three different official buildings here in Nassau just this morning. No one seems to be able to locate anyone from her family. Her mother is dead, and so are her grandparents. I know they came from the Bahamas. They migrated to Florida in nineteen seventy-five, right before her mother, Lisa, was born. All I know is that the grandmother was called Valentina Rojas and her husband was Augustin Rojas. Could you please try again? Please?"

The woman looked at me over her glasses, then exhaled. I could sense she didn't care much about having to do this, but I wasn't going to give up. We had been sent around to so many different public authorities; I couldn't even tell them apart anymore. No one seemed to be able to access the records. As soon as I mentioned how old they were, they all gave me that same look.

The woman glanced at the note where I had written the two names, then tried again, tapping with her long—very fake—fingernails clacking along the keyboard. I sighed, then looked at Emily. She was biting her nails, and I could tell she was about to lose hope. I had thought it would be easy to find her family, but as it turned out, it wasn't. I just really wanted her to find someone she was related to, but so far, we had been in the Bahamas for three days and still hadn't found a single soul. Nothing about this trip had been as easy as I had thought it would be. Emily and I had fought a lot, and the tension between us seemed worse than ever.

I sighed and rubbed my sweating forehead. It was hot in the building, as it had been in all the other public buildings. The Bahamians had AC, but it didn't seem as effective as the ones we had back home. I turned and looked at Emily, who didn't even want to look at me. This wasn't how it was supposed to go. This was supposed to be a trip of bonding for us, a trip where I made her feel loved like my mother had told me to. This was a trip for her to get better. But still, she was hardly eating, and she seemed more annoyed with me than ever. What was I doing wrong?

While the lady tapped on her computer—not putting very much effort into what she was doing—I wondered about my former colleague Mike Wagner and what we had just gone through. How he had been able to hide his true nature from us all while killing all those people. It was still so hard to comprehend. I had trusted him all my adult life while on the force. He had been a friend. I still couldn't fathom the things he had done. Who could I trust after this? Who did I dare to trust?

I could still see the rage in his eyes as I shot him in the forehead. It was the hardest decision I had to make in my life in uniform, but it had to be done. Still, it gave me nightmares, and during the day, I could drift off, thinking about him and that feeling that had rushed through me as I fired my weapon. It was so definite, so fatal. I kept wondering if there could have been another way to end it, whether I should have done something different.

My boss, Weasel, head of the Cocoa Beach Police Department, had thought it was an excellent idea that I took some time off while they closed the case back home, but even though I was far away, I had brought it all with me emotionally, and I couldn't help but feel devastated from time to time.

"I'm sorry," the woman said and looked at me. "They don't exist in any of our records."

"You mean to tell me they never had a driver's license? They never registered to vote or even bought a house?"

The lady lifted her eyebrows and gave me a look to let me know she was getting tired of this conversation.

"It was in seventy-five they left," she said. "That was a long time ago."

"And the last name? You don't get anyone else showing up with that last name when you search?"

She shook her head, but I could swear she had no idea.

"So, no one is named Rojas on any of the islands?" I asked, sensing myself growing angrier. This lady seemed not to care one iota.

"I can't find them," she said.

"Come on. This girl just wants to find her relatives," I said, resigned. "Her family is Bahamian."

The lady gave Emily a look like she was sizing her up. "Don't look very Bahamian to me," she said with that strong accent most of them had to their English.

"Yeah, well, of course not. She grew up in Florida," I said.

"Don't think she's got much Bahamian in that skinny body of hers," the lady said and shook her head. "Bahamians are fat. We like to eat." Then, she laughed and jiggled behind the counter, and I sighed once again. It had been the same everywhere we went. No one seemed to be able to find Emily's family, and they didn't seem to understand the urgency. The idea in itself was an abomination to them. They all lived by that island mentality where you wait till tomorrow to worry about the problems while throwing around annoying sayings like *We Bahamians are too blessed to be stressed*. It was all very great and Zen-like if you were on vacation. I'm sure the tourist loved the laid-back attitude, and under normal circumstances, I probably would too, but when you wanted something done, it didn't really work.

I grabbed the paper where I had written Emily's grandparents' names and gave the lady an annoyed look.

"Come on, Em. Let's get out of here."

We walked toward the front door, Emily following close behind me. I put a hand on the glass part of the door and then turned to look at her.

"I'm sorry. I really thought this would be a lot easier. I mean, there are less than four hundred thousand people in the Bahamas. How hard can it be to find someone?"

"Just let it go, Jack," she said, and we walked outside into the bright sunlight. "Maybe it was a mistake even to come here."

Jack? I hated when she called me that. I was her dad. I had never felt like anything else to her, yet she insisted on calling me by my name lately.

I paused. "A mistake? Is that what you think?"

She sighed, deeply. "Listen, Jack."

I cringed.

"I know you've brought me here because you think this will somehow fix me, that you can fix me or maybe solve me like one of your little mysteries, but I am not broken. I am not yours to fix."

Emily stared at me, her nostrils flaring. Her words felt like punches to my gut.

"You don't want to be fixed?"

Emily answered with an annoyed growl. "You just don't get it, do you?"

I shook my head. "No. I don't. I really don't."

She stepped forward. "I am happy, Jack. I am happy the way things are. Being skinny makes me happy. Not eating makes me happy. Getting on the scale and realizing I have lost more weight makes me happy. I like the way I look. I enjoy it. It's all I ever wanted. I hated being fat; I hated looking like a whale in seventh grade. Now, I don't. Now, I look good in my pictures when I post on Instagram. I feel good about myself. I don't want to get better because what you think is better is not my idea of a good life. I am a grown-up now, Jack. I can make my own decisions, and this is it. This is my decision. Call it an eating disorder, call it anorexia, call me crazy; I don't care. This is it, this is me now, Jack. "

I swallowed. I felt tears appear in my eyes. I never knew it was this bad. Was that why nothing seemed to help with her? Because she wanted this? She liked it? But how was she going to get well then?

I was at a loss for words.

Emily took off down the stairs, her skinny stick-like legs poking out of her shorts, making her look like a skeleton. I couldn't believe that she wanted to look like that. Why couldn't she see how terrible it was? How awful she looked? Was that part of the disease? The doctors at the clinic I sent her to said so, but I had never stared into her eyes and seen it like that or even heard her express it this way before.

It completely startled me, and I felt paralyzed.

"You coming?" she asked as she reached the rental car in the parking lot. "I'm freezing."

It's ninety degrees and so humid I can hardly breathe, and you tell me you're freezing?

A tear escaped my eye and rolled across my cheek. I knew she was constantly freezing these days, but I also knew that it was because her body wasn't functioning properly. It wasn't able to keep itself warm, and soon her organs would begin to give out. They wouldn't be able to sustain what she was doing to herself for much longer.

I was running out of time.

"Excuse me?"

The voice coming from behind me startled me, and I turned around quickly to find a small grey-haired Bahamian woman standing behind me. She was holding a newspaper in her hand and held it out to me.

"I couldn't help overhearing you in there," she said and pushed the newspaper at me. "Here. This might help."

2

Bahamas, July 1977

She couldn't see anything. When the girl opened her eyes, there was total darkness and, for a few seconds, she completely panicked, thinking she had gone blind.

She was lying on a mattress of some sort. She could feel it underneath her, and she wondered for a minute if she was back home in her grandmother's house. But then she remembered. She remembered the men, the yelling men. And the boat, the big boat that she spent night after night on, while it made her sick to her stomach as it transported her to a destination foreign to her, but with promises of a better life. At least that was what her grandparents had told her it would be.

That was before they started to cough. After that, they barely spoke until they didn't even breathe anymore.

There were about twenty other people there in the bottom of the boat. So many of them laid down and never got up again. The girl watched them while she held her grandmother's limp hand in hers, pleading with her to wake up.

But she never did. She never made it to dry land. Neither did her grandfather. So, the girl had to leave the boat alone along with the few others who hadn't started to cough yet.

The girl cried when thinking about it and blinked her eyes, hoping it would make the darkness go away. She had done the same when they had shone flashlights in her face as she walked onto the ramp and off the boat. So many yelling voices, so many foreign men, such strange words emerging from their lips, words she didn't understand.

And then there was a woman.

The woman had been standing in the light of a streetlamp, a cigarette in the corner of her mouth, looking down at the girl. Then she had opened the girl's mouth, looked at her teeth, and pulled her shirt up to look at her stomach and back before nodding to the men holding her.

She had taken her with her. She had let her sit in the back of her truck while the strange landscape whooshed by, and the girl cried and called her grandmother's name into the night.

"¡Hola?" the girl now said into the darkness.

But no one answered. A long period of time went by, and the girl's eyes soon got used to the darkness. She realized then that she hadn't gone blind. There was a little bit of light coming from underneath a door at the end of the room, and soon the girl got up from the mattress and walked to it. She put an ear to the heavy wooden door and listened but could hear nothing. She grabbed the handle, but the door was locked. Yet the girl pulled at it while sobbing. She wanted to go back to the boat; she wanted to find her grandparents who were bound to have woken up by now. No one could sleep that long. Not even Uncle Pedro who always slept in when he came to visit at her grandmother's house.

The girl got tired of pulling at the door, then slid to the floor, feeling so scared and helpless.

The girl sat on her knees on the cold tiles and cried when suddenly there was a sound coming from the other side of the door. A scraping followed by the sound of hatches being opened.

The bright light coming from the other side as it was opened almost blinded the girl just as much as the flashlights had when she arrived in this strange country.

But as her eyes got used to the light, she realized it was the woman who was standing in front of her, wearing her long white dress. The girl first thought that she had died and gone to heaven and what was standing in front of her was an angel.

Little did she know at that point, but she had actually landed in hell, and the woman in front of her was the devil.

3

Nassau, Bahamas, October 2018

Back at the hotel room, Emily was lying on the bed watching TV, while I read the article the old woman had given me outside city hall. I kept reading it over and over again, making sure I understood it correctly. I was trying to determine if it was good news or bad news and how to tell Emily about it.

Emily soon grew tired of the TV and turned it off. She sat up straight and looked at me.

"So, you found out what it's all about yet?" she asked.

I took a deep breath, then leaned forward in the chair, not knowing quite how to tell her about it.

The room was small but had a nice view of the turquoise ocean and the white beach. When I booked it, I had believed we might be able to spend a few days just hanging out on the beach, maybe even with Emily's newly found relatives, but the way things were going, I feared there would be no time to relax. I was determined not to leave until I had found at least one person who was related to her, even if it meant spending every day of my two-week vacation tracking him or her down. I had promised Emily this since she was a young child and I adopted her when my partner Lisa died. While she was growing up, I kept telling her that one day we'd go and find her family in the Bahamas. Now the girl was nineteen. I know; better late than never, right? So many years had passed. I couldn't believe where all that time had gone. These days I sure missed Lisa and being able to ask her what to do about Emily. I couldn't help wondering how different Emily's life could have been, had I only been able to save Lisa's life that day. It still haunted me senselessly.

Why her and not me?

"I'm not sure," I said.

"What's it about?"

"It's about a trial a couple of months ago. This woman was convicted of having murdered a sixteen-year-old girl on the Western part of the island. The girl was on her way home from a boyfriend's house when she was attacked and killed. She was found in her family's pool the next morning."

Emily sat up and shrugged.

"So?"

I took a deep breath. "So, her name is Sofia Rojas. As in Valentina Rojas and her husband, Augustin Rojas."

Emily lifted her eyebrows. "Really? Rojas? That was the name of the girl who was murdered?"

I shook my head. "The woman who was convicted."

Emily left the bed and took a chair across from mine. "You think she might be my relative?"

"It's the only Rojas we've come across so far."

Emily scoffed. "With my luck, she's probably my relative and probably the only one around here. A murderer, ha. How fitting."

I put the article down on the small table between us. "She might not be a relative at all."

Emily took the newspaper. There was a picture of the woman on the cover, taken as she was brought out of the courtroom. It was not a very good one. The woman was covering her face with her arms as she was escorted through the crowd. It was hard to tell what she looked like. Next to it was a big school picture of the blonde girl who had been killed. Emily read the article and bit her lips. Then she put the paper down again. Our eyes met across the room.

"You think she might be worth a try?" she asked.

I shrugged. "Anything would be worth a try right about now. I have no other suggestions, do you?"

She glanced at the photo, then looked back up at me.

"Okay."

"Okay, what?" I asked.

She stood up.

"Okay, we go see her. Tomorrow."

I rose to my feet too. "That's a deal."

I looked at my watch. It was getting late. I would have to get up early and make some calls to find out how to get inside the prison.

"Now, I say we go down to the restaurant and get some dinner. They have grouper tonight."

Emily sat on the bed and grabbed the remote.

"You go," she said. "I'm staying here. There's a show I really want to watch. I'll eat later."

I grabbed the remote as she lifted it with the intention of turning on the TV, so I couldn't protest, the way she always did. I looked into her deep brown eyes that I had loved so much since she was just a young kid.

"What?" she asked, annoyed.

I shook my head.

"You're not fooling me. We had a deal, Emily. When we left, I told you I wanted to see you eat on this trip and, so far, you've hardly eaten anything. You're coming with me. And you're eating something."

Emily opened her mouth to protest, but I stopped her by lifting my finger. My mom had told me to stop trying to be Emily's friend and act like a dad instead, so this was me trying to act like a dad. I was sick of her excuses and her sneaky ways of trying to get out of eating, making up one silly lie after another.

"It wasn't a request. It was an order."

Emily gave me a look, then rolled her eyes, but she still followed me downstairs to the hotel's restaurant. She only had a salad, but I told the waiter to put chicken on it and watched her eat each and every bite, telling her she could go as slowly as she liked, but we weren't leaving till she finished the entire thing. So, she did. Reluctantly and while cursing me under her breath, but she did. She ate it all, and I watched her like a hawk all night, making sure she didn't go to the bathroom and throw it all up. If she did go in there, I listened intently, and she knew I would hear it.

She was not fooling me anymore.

4

Nassau, Bahamas, October 2018

Her Majesty's Prisons it said on the large green sign outside the tall fence. Behind it was a bunker-like building located outside of Nassau. I had often heard stories about how the prisons in the Bahamas were crowded and held a lot more inmates than they were designed for and that most criminals who came to serve time usually came out a lot more hardcore criminal than when they entered. I had also heard they didn't have separate prisons for women and men and the living conditions were often described as inhumane. Before coming today, I had read an article in a local paper just this morning telling me that there had been several recommendations to build a new prison. Unfortunately, those had not been heard and then the journalist added that *It now appears likely that before a new prison is built in The Bahamas, the sky will probably fall and there will be no need for a new prison anymore.*

I showed my ID and badge at the entrance, exploiting the fact that I was a police officer myself, even though I wasn't here on duty. It still worked. The guy behind the glass window looked at it, then at Emily by my side.

"She's my daughter," I said.

He gave me a confused glare.

"Adopted," I added.

He nodded and smiled widely the way many Bahamians did.

"I see."

"We made arrangements to see a prisoner, Sofia Rojas," I added and looked at my watch. I had called earlier this morning and made sure we could see her. To my surprise, it was a lot easier than I had anticipated.

The guy nodded eagerly and let us in. We were taken to a barren room with only two chairs, which I wasn't sure would be able to hold us and not break. Still, we sat down and waited, Emily tapping her foot nervously on the dirty floor. The stench in the prison was unbearable, and the guard leading us inside had offered us dust masks, but we refused. If the inmates and guards could survive breathing this air for years, maybe even decades, then we could endure it for a few hours. On our way inside, I saw human waste being taken out in large garbage bags; some of it even leaked onto the floor not far from where we were standing. The stench that seemed to cover the entire place wasn't only coming from the waste, but also from the generous applications of raw disinfectants poured on the floor everywhere. These were terrible conditions, not only for the inmates but also the guards. What was worse was the few who were in there who hadn't even been to trial yet. I remember reading about a guy who had been forgotten in this exact Bahamian prison for nine years, accused of a crime he didn't commit. Illegal immigrants that no one knew what to do about were rotting up in there. It was unbearable to think about.

The door opened, and two guards showed up, holding a woman between them. She was in chains and didn't look up at us.

I stood up. The guards let go of her, then one of them left, and the other stood by the door.

Emily gasped when the woman slowly lifted her head. She had been beaten terribly, and her right eye and cheek were completely swollen.

"Oh, dear Lord," I said.

I looked at Emily, wondering if this was too much for her.

Maybe I shouldn't have brought her here. I could have come by myself first.

I gave the woman my chair and helped her sit down. She looked up at me and tried to smile.

"Are you Sofia Rojas?" I asked and, as her eyes met mine, I was suddenly struck with an overwhelming sadness.

Her eyes, they were a true copy of my dear friend and partner Lisa's. It was just like looking at Emily's mom again.

5

Nassau, Bahamas, October 2018

Emily stared at Sofia, unable to take her eyes off her. I held my breath, thinking this had to be overwhelming for her, wondering how she would react. Right now, she was sitting in front of a woman who looked exactly like her mother. She was her true spitting image.

I could hardly believe it.

"Show her the picture," I said to Emily.

Cautiously, Emily held out a picture of her and her mother when she was just five-years-old toward Sofia and put it in her hands so she could look at it. Sofia stared at it, her hands shaking. Then she looked up at Emily with her head tilted slightly.

"This is Emily," I said and pointed at my daughter, then down at the girl in the picture. "And this is her mother, Lisa."

Sofia looked at the picture, then up at Emily again, a tear escaping her eye. Then she smiled and reached over to touch Emily's cheek.

"We think you might be related," I said. "I mean, you must be. You look just like her. Her grandparents' names were Valentina Rojas and Augustin Rojas. Do you know them?"

The woman looked up at me, then shook her head.

"But your name is also Rojas, and you look so much alike it's uncanny. Could you be a cousin maybe?"

The woman shook her head again.

"But certainly, you two must be related somehow," I said. "We've come here to find Emily's family, and we think you might be it."

Sofia answered with a shrug. I looked at the guard behind me, then back at her.

"Don't you understand English?"

Sofia nodded. I looked at the guard again, my eyes pleading for his help. But he remained cold faced. I returned to Sofia.

"We thought that maybe you could help us find more of Emily's family?" I asked. "Please? Do you have any family here? A mother and a father? Children maybe?"

Sofia turned her head away and stared emptily at the wall next to her while shaking her head.

"You shouldn't have come," she said with a sniffle. I could tell her swollen lip hurt when she spoke. "Go back to where you came from."

Sofia rose to her feet and turned to address the guard. "I'd like to go now."

"But…but we…"

I protested, but it didn't matter. The guard knocked on the door, and it was opened from the outside. I always hated the feeling of being at someone else's mercy this way, and them deciding when I left and whether I did. I had a slightly claustrophobic feeling growing inside of me until the door opened and the other guard came inside.

They grabbed Sofia by the shoulders and escorted her out. I sighed and looked at Emily with a shrug.

"I'm sorry, sweetie."

We were escorted out through the hallways, and Emily held her nose as we walked by one-man-cells with at least three or more prisoners in each of them. Some were sleeping on cardboard boxes, others eating while their cellmate relieved himself in what looked like a bucket in the corner. A rat greeted us as we turned a corner and Emily shrieked. I grabbed her hand in mine and kept it there till we reached the exit. I don't think I ever felt more relieved than when the gates were opened, and I once again smelled the fresh air.

"Remind me never to commit a crime while we're in the Bahamas," Emily said as we walked to our car.

"I am sorry, though," I said when we got inside. "I really thought she would talk to us."

"Maybe she didn't dare to?" Emily asked. "She looked scared."

I started the car. "I had really hoped we could get her to talk," I repeated and drove onto the road.

Driving in the Bahamas was somewhat of an accomplishment since the Bahamians drove crazily like their lives depended on them reaching their destination on time. It didn't fit very well with their laid-back attitude toward everything else, but you had to really keep an eye on each and every car in the street and be ready to blow the horn at any given moment. Sometimes, they simply honked because they saw someone they knew; sometimes, it was because they were happy, and other times, it was just to let you know they were coming around a corner. On top of it all, they drove on the left side of the road, which I was getting quite good at after a few days on the roads here. At least I thought so myself. I'm not so sure Emily shared that opinion as she would often shriek or scream while riding with me.

"It's okay, Jack," she said. "At least we found her. We actually found someone I was related to."

"I just wish we didn't have to find her in that awful place," I said.

Emily stared at the picture of her mother in her hand and then put it back in her pocket with a deep sigh.

"Let's go grab some ice cream," I said. "Like we used to when you were younger. Do you remember that?"

Emily gave me a look. I saw something in her eyes that I didn't know how to interpret. There was a fight going on inside of her. It was like the child in her wanted to eat that ice cream with me, really wanted to enjoy it, but the other part, the anorexic part told her she couldn't do it.

"Come on," I said. "One little ice cream won't hurt you."

I knew I was treading on dangerous water here since, so far, I had only been able to get her to eat salad and fruit for breakfast.

This would be a big step for her, one I wasn't sure she was ready to take yet. I was scared to be pushing her too much, but at the same time, I had to try. If I didn't ask, I would never get an answer, right? What if she said yes?

"I...I don't know Jack," she said and turned to look out the window.

I exhaled, a little disappointed. I put my hand on her shoulder. "It's okay, Emily. Maybe later, okay?"

She nodded but didn't look at me. I heard a light sniffle and wondered if she was crying.

6

Nassau, Bahamas, October 2018

It was happening again. The itch was back. The figure sitting in the car with the motor still running felt it while watching a group of locally well-known hookers standing outside the casino sharing a cigarette. The figure liked to watch the hookers, to see them waddle around in their misery.

But this individual wasn't there for the hookers. They weren't this person's targets. This person needed something else, something more shocking, more dangerous to satisfy the urgent demand that was growing inside.

The figure in the car pressed the accelerator down and soared past the girls into the night, whispering that they could *count themselves lucky* that they weren't the right type.

The car then drove through Nassau, slowly cruising past all the tourists by the cruise ships with the window open. The person was smiling at the sweet young girls in their summer dresses.

And that was when she showed up.

She was blonde and petite, and in good shape, not more than sixteen would be a good guess. Just got off the ship, walking with two of her friends toward town. They stopped for a few seconds and looked at all the tourist crap people were trying to sell them, but didn't buy any of it.

The car kept a distance but still close enough to watch their every move as they entered the Hard Rock Café. The person then parked the car and waited.

7

Nassau, Bahamas, October 2018

Nancy Elkington laughed lightly at her friend's joke. She was looking forward to getting back on dry land after many hours on the cruise ship. She was getting sick of people and *eat till you drop* buffets, not to mention overcrowded swimming pools. She was ready to get back on land and go shopping.

Nancy was so grateful that her parents had decided to let her take her two best friends with her on this trip since it would only have ended in total boredom without Melinda and Maria. At sixteen, the last thing you wanted to do was to hang out all day and night with your boring parents. And this afternoon, as the cruise ship docked in Nassau, her parents had told them they could go out and shop on their own, just the three girls. But they had to promise to stick together all the time.

"Where do you want to go first?" Melinda asked and looked at the map that the cruise ship had provided for them.

Men were yelling at them, asking if they wanted a taxi or a rickshaw to help them get across town, but the girls just waved at them dismissively and continued on foot.

"How stupid do they think we are?" Maria said.

"I know, right?" Melinda agreed. "Getting in a car with one of them just screams, *rape me*."

They passed a bunch of souvenir stands and stopped to look at some wooden sculptures, but then regretted it because the lady selling them wouldn't leave them alone and kept slinging prices at them.

"I'm hungry. There's a Hard Rock," Nancy said, spotting the sign in the distance. "Let's go eat there."

They all agreed and rushed on, leaving the woman in the stand disappointed. The girls laughed and swirled in their light summer dresses, enjoying the fact that they were able to wear them in October. Nancy hoped to get a good tan before the trip was over. Just enough to make them jealous back home.

As they spotted the café and started to cross the street, Nancy got the feeling that someone was watching her and turned to look. There was a group of people coming up behind her. They were obviously Americans, she could hear, and she breathed, relieved.

"Come on, Nance," Melinda yelled and grabbed her hand. The three of them hurried inside the café and ordered burgers while looking at the exhibit of famous artists' jackets and guitars and stuff like that. Nancy thought it was cool and took pictures of a pink cowboy hat that the sign said Madonna had worn while shooting a music video. Once the burgers were devoured, the girls decided it was time to go sightseeing, and they walked outside and into the street. As Nancy was about to cross it, she felt like she was being watched once again and paused. She looked up a small quaint street behind them. There were flags hanging from the windows in all colors.

"What's wrong?" Melinda said.

Nancy looked around her. There were lots of people in the streets, tourists mostly, and cars driving by, some playing loud music from open windows. In the background towered the big cruise ships like mountains.

"I don't know. I just keep having this feeling..."

"Well, stop it," Maria said and pulled her arm. "We're on vacation. We're supposed to have fun, remember?"

8

BAHAMAS, JULY 1982

"Could you give me the dress over there?"

The girl looked at the woman standing in front of her, then brought her the white dress on the hanger. The woman smiled and tousled her hair.

"Thank you."

The girl watched in awe while the woman put on the dress. She still believed she looked like an angel, even though the girl's cheek was sore from this morning's punches when she burned her toast; the girl couldn't help admiring her. She liked making the woman happy. If she did, the woman would smile and sometimes even sing. And then she wouldn't yell or even hit like she did when she was angry.

The girl had been at the house for five years now, and it didn't take her long to find out that The White Lady made the rules. Her husband traveled a lot—often to other houses they owned, the girl had been told—and never really cared much about what happened back at the house in the Bahamas. Meanwhile, The White Lady had taught the girl to understand English and trained her to cook and clean for her and help her out wherever it was needed. And ever since baby Dylan came too, shortly after the girl did, there had been a lot to do. The girl wasn't the only helper around the house, and she had learned that several of the women took care of the baby since The White Lady was way too busy to do it herself.

The girl's job was mostly to help out where she could, especially help Carla in the kitchen, and then play with the boy. Since The White Lady didn't care for him playing with other children, she often had the girl entertain him. When it was time for him to start school, The White Lady said she didn't want him to go to a real school and be with other children. She was afraid of the diseases he would meet, of the children and teachers and of how inferior the schools were. The girl overheard her tell the husband those things—one day when he was actually there—and since he didn't mind much what happened anyway, baby Dylan—who was no longer a baby, but an annoying five-year-old—began his homeschooling. Often, the girl would sit in the corner and listen in as his private teacher spoke, and that was how she learned how to read and write, which was more than you could say about Dylan, who never really listened much and would rather play with his trucks or go in the pool.

The girl thought he was being stupid, but that was just one of the emotions she felt when looking at him.

Since his mother was keeping the boy from socializing with other children, it soon made him timid, eccentric, and a little strange. Often, the girl would go with the nannies to the park close to the house and the nannies would pull him away when other children came to play with him, on The White Lady's orders. Once, the girl overheard The White Lady tell another mother that her child had tested in the genius range and that was why she didn't want him mingling with other children. That had made the girl laugh to herself. Dylan was many things, but he certainly was no genius.

A year later, The White Lady caught him peeking at the nannies when they were dressing. She then realized it might be time for him to hang out with other children and she selected a few that she believed it would be okay for him to be with. She paid their parents for the children to play with him and picked them up in the family's limousine. The first boy, Troy, who came to play walked down the hallway of the back-house, took one look at the doors, then pointed and said:

"How come all the doors have deadbolts on them—on the outside?"

After that, Troy was never invited to play with Dylan again.

9

Nassau, Bahamas, October 2018

Nancy felt sick to her stomach. They were walking in an indoor market between stands that sold souvenirs and clothing. The noise in there was unbearable. People were yelling at her from all sides, telling her to come to their shop and buy their hats or dresses or small wooden hand-carved turtles.

The other girls were walking ahead of her, while Nancy fought to keep up. She felt dizzy, and her stomach was cramping.

Maria stopped and looked back at her. "Are you okay, Nance? You look awful."

"Well, thank you very much," she said, moaning as she felt another pinch in her stomach.

"Do you think it might have been the food?" Maria asked while Nancy leaned against a stand with tie-dyed T-shirts.

"You want T-shirt, huh?" the lady standing next to it asked. "Very cheap. Very cheap."

Nancy looked at the pattern and felt even worse. Then she shook her head and staggered onward.

"It was probably that burger," she said, addressed to Maria. It was the only thing she had eaten since she landed on the island.

That and the soda she bought from that guy selling them outside the old church, but that was in a can.

"We also had those conch fritters, remember?" Maria added. "Down at the port. They did taste a little suspicious."

Nancy nodded. She didn't really care what it was, only how to get relief.

"I...I think I need to find a bathroom, fast," she said.

"I saw a sign over there for restrooms," Maria said and pointed. "I'll walk with you."

"No. It's okay," Nancy said. "You just go ahead. I'll catch up afterward. Just don't go too far, okay?"

Maria gave her a look.

"Are you sure? We'll just walk to the end of the market up there and then wait for you, okay?"

"That sounds fine," Nancy said absentmindedly. She had spotted the sign to the restroom and was staggering toward it, bending forward, holding a hand to her cramping stomach.

"Text me if you need anything," Maria yelled after her, concerned.

Nancy waved at her, not hearing—or caring—what she said, her eyes only focused on getting to the bathroom, fast. She pushed the door open and hurried inside a stall, then bent over and threw up into the toilet bowl, not even noticing the awful stench or closing the stall door.

Nancy threw up the burger, the conch fries, and the soda. Once her stomach was finally empty, she slid to the floor, drool running down her chin, panting for breath. She couldn't remember the last time she had felt this awful. The nausea subsided for just a moment, and that made her relax as she leaned her head back against the stall wall, closed her eyes, and breathed in.

She almost didn't hear the door to the restroom as it squeaked open.

10

Nassau, Bahamas, October 2018

Emily ate a small piece of chicken and even had a bite of one of my conch fries that I convinced her to taste, telling her that she simply couldn't have been in the Bahamas and not eaten conch fries.

Pleased with my accomplishments, I leaned back in my chair after dinner, drinking my beer and watching the next singer as she grabbed the microphone. It was karaoke night at the hotel and, much to my surprise, none of the singers who took the mike could carry a tune. Most of them were locals who came to hang out and sing, but it sounded so terrible that I considered taking my beer up to the room instead. Yet we stayed and made fun of them. It turned out to be something we could both laugh at.

"I am so sorry," I said after the third singer had left and we had stopped laughing.

"Why?" she asked. "You're not the one singing."

I chuckled. "That's not what I meant."

"What did you mean?" she asked. "What can you, the amazing Jack Ryder, everyone's savior, what can you possibly be sorry for?"

I exhaled. "For everything. For neglecting you. For not being able to save you."

She gave me a look, and I thought I saw the old Emily in there somewhere. Just for a brief second, then she was gone.

"I told you. I'm not yours to save. I'm happy, Jack."

I scoffed. I couldn't help myself. "Happy, huh?"

She nodded. "Yes, happy. I told you; being skinny makes me happy."

I could hardly breathe. Hearing her say stuff like that made me want just to grab her and shake some sense into her.

"Well, then, I'm sorry I couldn't find more relatives for you," I said, trying to take the conversation elsewhere.

She gave me a look, then leaned over as the next singer approached the mike on stage, and the DJ yelled something so loudly into his mike that it was impossible to understand.

"I read the article again," Emily said. "In the car and I thought about something."

"Yes?"

"Sofia worked for a family as a maid," she said.

I nodded. "The family whose daughter she killed."

Emily shook her head. "Maybe it's just a stupid idea."

"No, go ahead. It's better than no idea."

"I just thought that maybe if we went to them and talked to them, then maybe they could tell us something about her? Maybe they have some of her stuff? It said in the article that she lived with them. Maybe they have some pictures or anything that can tell me who she was or whether she has any relatives? Maybe they'll know where to search for her family?"

I stared at my daughter, a smile spreading. "That is actually a very good idea."

She made a face. "You hate it, don't you? I knew you would. It was just stupid."

"No. I just said I thought it was a great idea."

She wrinkled her nose. "You're just saying that to be nice. You do that a lot. I know you're afraid of making me sad, but please don't do me any favors."

I reached over and grabbed her bony hand.

"No. Emily, listen to me. I'm not kidding. I think we should do it. We'll go pay them a visit tomorrow, okay?" I shrugged. "What do we have to lose?"

11

Bahamas, October 2018

Nancy blinked her eyes. A bright light was shining in her face, and it made her feel sick. She sat up and looked around.

Where am I?

She was sitting on a couch. It was soft. In front of her was a round coffee table made from thick glass. All the furniture was very high-tech and expensive. Nancy's parents weren't rich, but she had been around wealthy people enough in her life to recognize an expensive couch when she saw one. The fabric alone felt amazing.

What am I doing here?

She tried to remember. She recalled the ship docking in Nassau, then she and the girls got off the boat and headed into town. Then they had the burger at Hard Rock, and then they went shopping. She had promised to bring back a souvenir for her boyfriend, Billy. She had been looking for a hoodie for him and maybe a similar one in a different color for her, when she fell sick, when she needed to go to…

The bathroom. I threw up and then…

Nancy gasped and rose to her feet. As she did, she felt dizzy again and had to sit back down. As she gathered herself, she remembered the door creaking open, then the steps that followed and soon stopped right behind her. She remembered gasping and turning to look just as a set of hands reached out for her. She vaguely remembered there being a car. She remembered screaming, but she also remembered her mouth being covered and then there was something, a prick against her skin. Then dizziness followed before everything went black.

Panicking, she looked around her and realized the room she was in had no windows. It was very expensively decorated with paintings on the walls—that didn't seem to be copies—and designer lamps hanging from the ceiling. But there was something missing.

A door. No matter where Nancy looked, there was no door.

"Mom?" she asked into the vast space, hoping and praying she was somewhere back at the ship in one of the more expensive suites. Maybe someone had taken care of her while she was sick?

"Dad?"

Nancy whimpered as she turned around once more to see if she could find a door, but there simply wasn't one. Finally, she managed to get to her feet and walked to the stone wall behind the couch and felt it. There wasn't a crack in it to tell her this was the exit. There was no door handle or anything she could pull.

How did I get in here if there is no door?

Suddenly, the air felt tight in her throat, and Nancy gasped. What was this place? What was she doing there?

Nancy knocked on the wall as if she believed it would somehow magically open. She walked to the middle of the room and stared up at the ceiling.

"Hello? Can anyone hear me? Hello? HELLO?"

12

Bahamas, July 1983

Before Gabrielle came along, the girl had never thought about running away since this was all she knew. She had believed she belonged here, that this was her home, and that The White Lady took care of her because her grandparents had died.

It wasn't until one of the newly-arrived grown women, Gabrielle, started to talk about getting away that the girl even considered it a possibility. But where would she go?

Gabrielle couldn't stop talking about it, about how they were being kept there against their will, that this wasn't what she had paid all her mother's savings to get to. She had been promised America, a job, and freedom. This wasn't that at all. This was just another prison. This was no better than back home.

"They're exploiting you all," she said, pointing her finger at each of them while they sat on the brown tiles in the kitchen. "Keeping you as slaves."

The girl didn't quite understand what Gabrielle was talking about, but the more she listened to her stories about foreign places, the more the girl started to remember how her grandparents had been dreaming of the same thing. How they too had talked with feverish eyes about the USA and how everything would be better once they got there. How the girl would see her real mother and father.

Being ten years old now, the girl suddenly understood a lot more and started to dream herself. Was there really a life outside of this place, a life where no one would beat you if you made the coffee too strong or dropped a cup on the floor? A life without constantly fearing The White Lady's wrath?

"I'm telling you," Gabrielle, said. "I'm leaving. Tomorrow. Anyone who wants to come with me is welcome."

"It's dangerous," Carla said.

The girl had always liked Carla. She took good care of her and washed her wounds that time when The White Lady had scratched her with her long nails and made long bloody stripes on her back. The wounds had become swollen afterward and infected, probably because of dirt and bacteria from underneath her nails, Carla had explained, then called her a disgusting monster.

The other women in the kitchen nodded, agreeing with Carla.

Gabrielle scoffed. "You're all just cowards. Well, suit yourselves. Stay here for the rest of your life if you like. See if I care. I'm getting out of here."

That night, the girl lay awake on her mattress. Her wide-open eyes were watching the lizard crawling on the ceiling while wondering with a pounding heart whether she too should take the chance and get away from there, find herself a life of freedom away from The White Lady and all her rules. She could pursue the dream her grandparents had and maybe find her real parents. For years, she had waited for them to come find her where she was, but as she grew older, she slowly realized that maybe they didn't know where she was. Maybe they weren't coming after all.

Maybe she'd have to find them herself.

13

Lyford Cay, Bahamas, October 2018

I had never seen such wealth in my entire life. Not even in Fort Lauderdale where I grew up, not in Miami or any of the suburbs, or even in West Palm Beach. This was out of this world. It was so extravagant that it made me feel sick to my stomach.

The family that Sofia had served with lived in Lyford Cay, a gated community on the western tip of New Providence Island. It was hard to imagine that this was the same island that also housed the capital, Nassau. It was considered to be one of the world's wealthiest and most exclusive neighborhoods, known to house billionaires and playboys, where they could live their press-shy lives unnoticed.

According to newspaper articles—and Google—Ella Maria Chauncey's family were shipping heirs, or at least the mother was, while her husband used to be a New York financier before they met. Now, it was commonly known that Mr. Chauncey mostly handled golf equipment and champagne bottles.

I had called ahead and spoken to the father, and he told me he'd put my name on the list at the gate. I had to admit, I felt slightly nervous as we parked the rental car in the driveway that was big enough to be called a highway where I came from.

"Why are you sweating so much?" Emily asked me as we got out of the car. "Your shirt is all soaked."

"It's hot," I said.

"You didn't sweat like that yesterday, and it was just as hot."

I pulled my shirt from my sweaty chest to get some air inside it. "What can I say? Rich people make me nervous."

Emily chuckled. "You're married to one."

"It's not the same, and you know it. Shannon is a singer, famous and rich, yes, but nothing like these people. She is not demanding and entitled the way rich people usually are. She doesn't set up standards so high you can't reach them. She's human. These people aren't."

Emily chuckled again. "They still put their pants on the same way as we do. One leg at a time."

"I'm not sure people like this even wear pants, Em," I whispered as we approached the front door.

"How are they, by the way?"

"Who?" I asked.

"Shannon and the kids? Back home?"

It was the first time Emily had asked about them. I had been calling them each morning and evening, but she hadn't seemed interested in knowing how they were. I was guessing she really needed the break from them. It was a little much and a little crazy around the house with five young kids and a puppy, but that was my reality. And Shannon's. I just hoped she was handling it well. I worried about her. Of course, I did. She had only been off the painkillers since August. I feared this was too much for her, being alone with all those kids. But she had assured me she could do it.

"They're great," I said. "Shannon's a little overwhelmed, but she's doing well. I spoke to Nanna earlier, and she even says Shannon is doing awesome."

"She didn't use that word," Emily said.

"Of course not. She said she was getting by. That's a lot coming from your grandmother on the subject of Shannon. You know it is."

Emily chuckled again. "Sure is."

I gave her a satisfied look, then turned to face the door just as it was opened.

14

Lyford Cay, Bahamas, October 2018

We were led through the huge hall and into what might have been a living room, one of many, I suspected, in a mansion like this. The black woman showing us the way nodded politely toward the other end of it, where a white man came walking toward us. He was wearing a golfing outfit and looked like he was about to leave.

"Hello," I said and approached him, stretching out my hand. "I'm Jack Ryder. We called earlier?" I made sure to keep out the detective part—once again since I had also done it on the phone—so he wouldn't be nervous. I had no jurisdiction here in the Bahamas. I was here on a private matter, so it wasn't important.

"You must be Mr. Chauncey?"

The man nodded and shook my hand. Much to my surprise, he didn't seem as snobbish as I had expected, and I was able to relax my shoulders.

"Yes, yes, welcome. Now, how can I be of help?" he asked. "It was regarding Sofia, right?"

I nodded and pulled Emily forward. "First of all, I am so sorry for your loss. I can't even imagine how…"

Mr. Chauncey stopped me. He held a hand to his face, shook his head, and sat down on an armchair behind him with a deep exhale. We sat on the couch in front of him and, as I looked closer, I could now see the deep grief in his eyes. I had seen it so many times before in my job, and still, it almost made me lose it every time. The thought of losing a child was simply too unbearable to me. I had many kids, but none to spare. I wouldn't be able to go on living. I don't think I could. I thought about the twins back home and then about Tyler and Betsy Sue and Angela. I put my hand on top of Emily's and squeezed it, worrying about her and whether I would end up losing her.

I wasn't going to survive it. It was as simple as that.

"I'm sorry, Mr. Chauncey…" I said. "I didn't mean to…"

He held a hand up. He was regaining his façade, something I suspected he was very good at. He had to be in this environment, right?

"It's all right. I still get emotional when talking about…her… about Ella, but…it's been seven months, for crying out loud. I should be able to…" he stopped himself and clenched his fist, then placed it in front of his mouth while forcing back the tears. It was an unbearable sight. Almost broke my heart.

Outside the window, I spotted the pool in the back facing the ocean. I knew from the article that was where they had found the girl the next morning.

Mr. Chauncey clapped his hands. "All right. Now, what about Sofia? What did you want to know?"

"My daughter here…" I pointed at Emily.

Mr. Chauncey gave me a look.

"Well, she is adopted," I explained. I was used to that reaction. "I adopted her when her mother died. She is looking for her relatives and, well…to make a long story short, we believe Sofia was related to her mother."

"I do see the resemblance," Mr. Chauncey said and kept looking at Emily.

"Yes, Sofia is the spitting image of Emily's mother, so we thought they must be related. When we went to visit her in jail, she wouldn't speak to us, so we hope…well, we thought maybe you could shine some light on this for us. Do you know if she has any relatives around here?"

Mr. Chauncey looked at me, surprised. "You don't know?"

I shook my head. "No?"

Mr. Chauncey smiled and got up. "Give me a second."

15

Lyford Cay, Bahamas, October 2018

I watched as Mr. Chauncey walked out and then came back, holding his arm around a young girl, a little younger than Emily, but otherwise close to her spitting image.

I rose to my feet.

"This here is Sydney," Mr. Chauncey said. "She's Sofia's daughter. She's lived with us since she was born. Sofia worked for us back then and so, when she was arrested, we decided to let Sydney stay. She is, after all, like a daughter to us and we would hate to see her in the streets."

"That's…that's awfully big of you considering what her mother did..." I said, feeling a sudden deep respect for this man. Her mother had murdered their only daughter, and yet they had decided to let the girl stay even though her very face reminded them of what her mother had done. I was impressed with their compassion, to say the least.

"Kids around here don't stand a chance if they end up in the streets," he said, while the young girl studied both of us closely. Mostly Emily.

"After all, she can't help what her mother did," Mr. Chauncey continued. "We're making sure she gets an education, so maybe she can reach above her mother's poor standards and judgment."

I nodded and smiled, then reached out my hand toward Sydney. "I'm Jack Ryder, and this young lady here beside me is Emily. I think you two are related."

The girl gave Emily a shy smile. Emily reached out her arms and pulled her into a hug. It was an emotionally loaded moment, and I could see how badly Emily's legs were shaking beneath her.

"Do you mind if they spend a little time together?" I asked. "We've been looking for relatives for days. This is really our first breakthrough."

He shook his head. "Not at all. Feel free to stay as long as you want." He glanced at his watch. "Now…I have a tee time in a few minutes, but Rosie will make sure you have everything you need. She's the one who showed you in."

"Is Mrs. Chauncey home?" I asked.

"No."

I smiled, forced. Mr. Chauncey's eyes had avoided mine when I mentioned Ella's mother, and I detected that things weren't the way they were supposed to be between them. It was only natural with all they had been through. Losing a child could destroy any marriage, no matter how strong it was.

"Naturally. But there was one other thing I wanted to ask of you before you leave."

"Yes?"

"Sofia Rojas. Do you know how she was related to Valentina Rojas and Augustin Rojas? Have you heard of them before maybe? They immigrated to the US in nineteen seventy-five from the Bahamas."

He shook his head. "I really wouldn't know. Sofia has worked for us for many years, but I have never met any of her family."

I thanked Mr. Chauncey for his time and watched him leave, while the two girls had already taken off. I spotted them out on the patio where Sydney was showing Emily around. I let them have their privacy and sat down on another of the many couches, pulled out my phone and called Shannon, responding to a deep desire to let her know how much I loved her.

16

BAHAMAS, JULY 1983

They took Dylan with them to the park the next morning. Carla, Gabrielle, and the girl. The White Lady had a hard time finding decent friends who would play with the boy, even though she offered to pay their parents. The few children who were good enough for his mother didn't like coming to his house, and Dylan was growing increasingly more and more lonely. The White Lady always asked the girl to hang out with him, so that's what she did most of the time. It wasn't too bad, she thought as she ran after him on the playground, playing Tag. Even if looking at the boy often filled her with more rage than she could contain in her young body. She knew it wasn't him she was angry with; it was his mother, The White Lady. But she couldn't help seeing her in the boy's face.

"You can't catch me," he now yelled and blew raspberries at her. "You can't catch me. You're too slow."

The girl hurried up and ran after him, running behind the slide, then grabbed him by the shirt. She pulled him back forcefully, and the boy ended up on his back, crying.

The girl stood above him, staring down at him, not even caring one bit that the boy was crying. Carla and Gabrielle didn't care either. No one usually did when The White Lady wasn't around. It was their little revolt against the woman who held them all as prisoners.

The girl stared at the boy, relishing in his pain and whining, almost enjoying it, sensing how the hairs on the back of her neck stood up and how overwhelmingly satisfying it was to see him lie there completely defenseless.

"I'm doing it," she heard Gabrielle yell. She and Carla were arguing loudly, and the girl knew what it was about.

"Don't, Gabby. You know it won't end well," Carla argued, pleading with her to stay. "Where will you go? This is a gated area. How will you get past the walls?"

"I'll jump in the ocean and swim down the shore," Gabrielle said.

"You'll get caught; you know you will. Someone will see you and bring you back. This is an island; there is nowhere to go. What if the police find you, huh? Then what will you do?"

"You can't stop me, Carla."

The girl watched them argue with her nostrils flaring in agitation, wondering what to do. She had thought about it all night long. She wanted to go with Gabrielle when she left. She wanted to see the Promised Land and not stay trapped here forever. Somewhere out there behind the walls that surrounded all the houses was another world, and that world housed her parents, her real mom and dad.

The girl looked down at Dylan, who was still crying, then lifted her foot and gave him a deep kick in the stomach before she took off, Dylan wailing behind her.

"Gabrielle. I'm coming with you," she yelled. "Wait for me!"

"No!" Carla yelled. She turned her head toward the girl, her nostrils flaring, then reached out and grabbed the girl's hand. Carla shook her head violently. "I'm not letting you do this. You're staying here; you hear me?"

"No," the girl said. "I want to go with her. I want to go away and find my parents."

Carla kept shaking her head, holding onto the girl's hand,

showing incredible strength. The girl fought with all she had to get loose, but by the time Carla finally let go of her hand, Gabrielle was long gone. The girl stared in the direction where she had disappeared, a tear escaping her eye and rolling down her cheek.

"Why would you do that?" the girl cried.

"You be happy now. I just saved your life," Carla said. Carla's hand then grabbed her shoulder and pulled her.

"Come on," Carla said. "Grab the boy. We need to get home."

17

Lyford Cay, Bahamas, October 2018

They were inseparable. I hated to have to split them apart, but after two hours, I felt like we were overstaying our welcome and I began preparing myself to tell Emily it was time to go back to the hotel.

The housekeeper, Rosie, stood in the doorway of the living room, constantly staring at me, and I was getting quite uncomfortable. I got the feeling she didn't like us being there. Or maybe she wanted to talk to me but didn't dare to. I couldn't quite figure it out. Just like I couldn't figure out why I felt so uncomfortable in her presence. Maybe it was the concept of housekeepers or the fact that she was black, and I felt like some colonist from back in the day. But as her eyes had lingered on me for long enough, I finally got up. I nodded politely to Rosie, who didn't react even though our eyes met, then walked outside through the sliding doors.

I found the girls sitting on a porch swing by one of the pools, chatting and laughing. I had to stop and listen for a few seconds, enjoying every second of seeing my daughter happy.

"It's time to go," I finally said, approaching them on the swing.

Emily gave me a sad look. "Really?"

"Yes."

Emily gave Sydney a big hug and then handed her one of her necklaces that she always wore. Sydney took it, then hugged her again.

Back in the car, we approached the security guard at the gate. Emily was very quiet as we drove back onto the big road outside of the massive walls. She had her head turned away from me, watching the scenery as we drove by it. It was quite beautiful with the turquoise water on one side of us, but I hardly noticed. I wanted to ask Emily about Sydney and what they talked about, but I didn't want to pry or risk saying something that made her sad. So instead, we ended up driving back to Nassau in silence.

It wasn't until I drove up in front of the hotel and parked that she finally opened up to me. It wasn't at all what I had expected to come out of her mouth.

"She didn't do it."

I looked at Emily, surprised. "What?"

Emily's eyes met mine. There was a deep sadness in hers.

"Her mom. She didn't do it."

I shook my head. "Sofia?"

"Yes, Sofia. She didn't kill Ella Maria."

I exhaled. "Emily. Of course, her daughter will say that her mom is innocent."

Emily shook her head. "No. It's true. She didn't do it. I believe her. She told me she couldn't have killed her."

"How? Does she have any evidence?" I asked.

Emily shook her head. "I don't know. But I believe her, Dad, I really do."

I swallowed, hard. *Dad.* Emily was suddenly calling me dad. She grabbed my arm with both of her bony hands.

"Without her mother, Sydney has no one. You have to help them. You're the only one who can."

"But, Emily…there is no way I can…"

"Yes, you can. You're the only one who can."

"Emily. We're in a different country. I have no jurisdiction here. I have no right to…"

"If you were a private investigator, you could, couldn't you? I know you can't make any arrests or anything like that, but you can investigate. No one can prevent you from doing that, can they?"

I sighed and rubbed my forehead. The girl was right. No one could stop me if I wanted to investigate.

"Please, Dad? Please?" she asked, her eyes pleading with me. "We still have a week and a half here and nothing else to do."

I closed my eyes and then opened them again.

"I guess I could look into it."

18

Bahamas, October 2018

Nancy was sitting on the beach when her boyfriend, Billy, came up to her and placed a wet kiss on her lips. He was still in his trunks, and his hair was wet. Nancy closed her eyes and enjoyed the kiss, wondering if it had all been a dream, a nightmare. The stomach bug, the restroom, the car, and the strange room with no windows or doors.

When she opened her eyes again, she looked into another set of eyes, but they weren't Billy's.

Nancy screamed and sat up, realizing she was back in the room. The person in front of her grinned from ear to ear.

"W-who are you?" Nancy gasped and sat up.

"Does it matter?" the person asked, leaning forward and almost whispering the words into her face.

"W-where am I? Why are you keeping me here?"

The person reached out a hand and started to caress Nancy's cheek. The gesture made Nancy's blood freeze.

"Such a pretty girl. I did well in choosing you. You're gonna be so beautiful on all the newspaper covers."

Nancy pulled back. "Let me out of here."

The person shook their head, then reached out a hand and grabbed Nancy's throat and started to press. Nancy gasped for air while the person, with a smile, held her throat until she was almost out of air before letting go. Nancy sank to the floor, coughing and gasping, then crawled backward, almost crabbing her way across the carpet. She then stood to her feet and stumbled away from the strange creature, falling once, then getting up again, staggering toward the wall, searching for a place to hide, but finding nothing, not even a closet. There was a restroom at one end of the room, but that had no doors or windows either. No escape.

Like a spider, the figure jumped down in front of her, stretching out their arms, laughing, reaching out, almost grabbing her, but missing as she lunged to the side, then ran to the other wall across the room.

The person chuckled. "You do realize there is nowhere to run, right?"

Nancy answered with a whimper. Panic was spreading inside her. The look in the person's eyes terrified her. The person approached her. Nancy stared around her, still looking for a way out. There had to be one, right? There was a way in. The person had entered somehow while she slept.

"There's nowhere you can hide, nowhere you can run, pretty girl," the person said.

"Please…let me go," Nancy pleaded, even though she knew it was useless.

As the figure leaped for her again, Nancy ran to another wall, gasping for air, but as she passed the person, she felt a hand reach out and grab hers, then pull her back forcefully. Nancy screamed as she flew through the air and landed on the floor, knocking her head into the tiles. When she opened her eyes again, the person was hovering above her, then lifted a fist into the air and slammed it into her face over and over again until she tasted her own blood.

PART II

19

Nassau, Bahamas, October 2018

"I'm just asking to take a look at it."

I smiled. The man sitting in front of me was scrutinizing me.

"And I'm just asking why you need to take a look. This case is closed. Killer was found. We haven't asked for your help. We haven't asked for American help with this case."

I sighed and leaned back in the worn-out chair where they had told me to sit. The man behind the desk was Commissioner Maycock. He was looking at me like I was a child that he was scolding. Behind him hung a sign showing an emblem reading ROYAL BAHAMAS POLICE FORCE with a small crown on top.

"We don't want any trouble," he said.

"I know," I said. "But the girl was American. I would like to take a look at her autopsy report, please."

Commissioner Maycock exhaled and leaned back in his old creaking chair. Everything at the police station seemed so old and in dire need of renovation. The only thing that seemed impeccable were their uniforms. The Commissioner was in a beige one that was perfectly ironed. He had a tie underneath the buttoned-up jacket and was wearing an old-fashioned stiff hat with a red ribbon. He didn't look very comfortable or even practical if he needed to run after a suspect, but he looked very presentable, I had to admit. The man in front of me carried many medals on his chest, and I knew he was important.

"We don't want any trouble," he repeated like he didn't believe I had heard him the first time.

I nodded. "I know. I just want to take a look."

"Case is closed. The murderer is in jail. Everything is in order. We can move on now," he said.

I smiled. "Yes, and that is all very good police work, I'm sure. I just…well, I have another case that is similar to this one," I lied. "And there are some details I would like to take a look at if you don't mind."

The little white lie seemed to do the trick. I was now asking the man for his expertise and not judging him to find fault. It made the commissioner thaw and even smile.

"Well, yes, of course."

The big man behind the small desk leaned forward and stretched out his hand toward me. We shook, and he handed me the report, just as one of his deputies came rushing toward him, a round hat in his hand tugged neatly into the side of his uniform. There was an almost military precision to the way he acted that didn't quite fit in with anything else around us.

"Sir, we have an issue."

"What is it, Corporal?"

The corporal changed his position and leaned forward, bending down toward the commissioner. He was sweating heavily.

"Someone is here. Filing a missing person's report. For a teenager."

The commissioner looked up at the corporal. "A missing teenager?"

The corporal nodded. "Yes, sir. She is missing from the cruise ship. Parents are American."

The commissioner let out a deep exhale. "Not again. Have they searched the entire ship?"

The corporal nodded, wiping off sweat with the back of his

hand. "She's been missing since last night. The parents say she went onshore with two friends to go shopping and that she disappeared at the Straw Market. She was last seen walking into a restroom. No one's seen her since."

"And she's American, huh?" The commissioner looked at the corporal, who nodded. Then his eyes landed on me. "Looks like we'll be needing your assistance after all, Detective Ryder."

20

Nassau, Bahamas, October 2018

There was a lot of commotion at the front desk. I could hear voices yelling at one another and recognized the worry and anxiety in the voice of the man I assumed was the father of the missing girl.

The commissioner walked out, and I followed closely behind. "Mr. and Mrs. Elkington," he said and reached out his hands toward them. His corporal had told him their names on their way out, and I noticed it brought comfort to the parents that he at least knew who they were. This wasn't his first time dealing with parents who had lost their child when vacationing in Nassau.

"I am Commissioner Maycock. My corporal here tells me your daughter is missing?"

Mr. Elkington looked at us with flustered eyes. His wife was standing one step behind him, her face torn in anguish.

"We've looked everywhere," he said and glanced quickly back at his wife like he wanted her to confirm. She nodded in agreement, and he continued. "Sh-she went with her friends to the market to buy…"

"A shirt for her boyfriend," Mrs. Elkington took over. Her cheeks were blushing in agitation. "They ate at the Hard Rock Café, then went to the market afterward. That's where she disappeared. She never came back to the ship with the others."

Mrs. Elkington squirmed when saying the last part, leaning forward like her stomach was cramping.

"We've been everywhere, talked to everyone, but no one seems to care," Mr. Elkington took over. "All they keep telling us is that she'll show up eventually and that it happens all the time."

"It does," the commissioner said. "People get lost, or they stay out partying with people they met. Sometimes, they're sleeping somewhere. With men they've met. We even had one girl who went missing, and we searched all over for her, but she turned out to still be on the ship sleeping in a guy's cabin. They were so drunk they had slept through the entire ordeal."

Mr. Elkington stepped forward, his cheeks blushing. "I don't care if it happens often. These people are not my daughter. Nancy would never do anything like that."

"That's what all parents say," the commissioner said.

"Our daughter is missing," Mrs. Elkington said. "Why won't you take it seriously? Our ship leaves tonight. We need to find her."

The commissioner nodded. "I know. And to show you that we do take this very seriously, we have called in special assistance today." He turned and looked at me, then signaled for me to step forward. "Detective Jack Ryder from Florida is here to assist you and find your daughter, isn't that right, Detective?"

I felt confused. Two sets of very hopeful yet anxious eyes were fixated on me. I thought about Emily, who I had left back at the hotel. How was she going to feel about this? I was, after all, on this vacation to help her and be with her, not to work. But still. How could I refuse to help those poor parents in their time of need? That wasn't something I was very likely to do. I felt slightly ambushed, but that wasn't the parents' fault. They just needed all the help they could get right now, and apparently, I was it.

I nodded and stepped toward them, reaching out my hand.

"Yes, that's correct. I'll help you look for your daughter."

21

Nassau, Bahamas, October 2018

I called Emily from the car and filled her in on the details. She wasn't too fond of the idea of me being dragged into a case while we were supposed to spend time together, and while I was supposed to focus on helping Sofia, but I think she understood.

"She probably just wandered off, and we'll find her in a couple of hours," I said to her, trying to sound reassuring. "Meanwhile, keep digging into those articles we found. See if anything stands out; make a note of anything that comes off as strange to you."

"Okay," she said just as I stopped the car in front of the Straw Market and we hung up.

I put the phone in my pocket, then got out and met with the Elkingtons outside the entrance. They were with an officer from the Royal Bahamian Police, who had driven them there from the station. We walked inside, and I was immediately overwhelmed. So many colors, so many people, and so much noise. Every little stand was packed with so many things you could buy, funny cups, hand-carved souvenirs, hats, scarves, and T-shirts. So many bags and small trinkets, I became almost exhausted just trying to find my way through.

I followed the Elkingtons across the market, zigzagging our way through the crowds of people, going toward the restroom where Nancy had last been seen by her friend Maria.

Her parents stopped outside. The mother opened the door and peeked in, then nodded to me.

"It's okay. There's no one in there. You can go in."

I walked past her into the restroom and closed the door behind me. I opened the first stall and looked inside while holding a hand to my mouth and nose to shield myself from the terrible stench. You had to really need to go in order to use this restroom, in my opinion. But that fitted well with the description they had given me. Nancy's friend Maria had told the parents that Nancy felt sick to her stomach and that she had rushed to the restroom. That was why she had left the others, even though her parents had told them always to stick together, no matter what. But when you had to go, you had to go.

I opened the second stall, and it smelled even worse than the first. I used my sleeve to cover my mouth and nose while peeking in. The toilets were old and looked rusty. There was no seat on any of the bowls. I turned to walk away when I noticed something was wrong with the door to the stall. The door couldn't close properly and seemed to have taken a blow to it. Plus, there was something else. Scratch marks on the bottom of it. Like nails had been digging into the paint. Like someone had tried to hold on.

Because she was being dragged away.

I shook the thought, then knelt by the door. I looked at the floor beneath the door and spotted three drops of blood that had dried up on the tiles. I looked around, then spotted the trash can next to the sink. I walked to it and looked inside, then using two fingers, pulled out a purse from underneath used tissue paper and banana peels.

The door opened behind me, and Mrs. Elkington came in.

"You find anything?"

"Guess it's to our advantage that they don't clean this place very often," I said out loud, then turned around and showed her the purse.

"Does this belong to your daughter, by any chance?"

Mrs. Elkington didn't have to answer. Her sudden pallor and the hand clasped to her chest were more than enough.

22

Bahamas, July 1983

It didn't take long before it was discovered that Gabrielle had run away. It was maybe two hours after they had returned from the playground when The White Lady started to ask questions. She started with Carla, whom she confronted in the kitchen.

"Where is she?"

Carla was bent over the stove, making her famous *Bandeja Paisa* that The White Lady loved so much. She froze as she came up behind her and asked the question. The girl was sitting in the corner when it happened. Her heart sank when she saw how Carla winced.

"I said, where is she?" The White Lady repeated. She was wearing a completely white dress, as usual, and a white scarf around her head to cover her hair so the sun wouldn't ruin it. The White Lady loved her hair and went to the hairdresser many times a month to make sure it was always perfect. The girl didn't quite understand why she insisted on covering it up when she spent so much money making it beautiful, but then again, there was so much she didn't quite grasp about her.

When Carla didn't answer, The White Lady grabbed her by the shoulder and pulled her till she faced her. Carla stood with her head bent when the slap fell, then another, and then another. The girl saw it happen and shrieked from her corner.

"Where is she, stupid girl? Where is she?" the lady continued, still hitting Carla till she fell to her knees, her ear bleeding.

The girl stood to her feet, staring at them with eyes wide.

"Did she run away, huh? Did she?"

Carla whimpered and held a hand to her head, expecting another blow to fall from The White Lady's strong hands.

"Did she run?" she asked again, almost yelling this time.

Finally, Carla nodded.

The answer didn't please The White Lady, and she grabbed the cheese grater lying on the counter next to her, then grabbed Carla's arm and started to grate her skin.

"Where did she go? Tell me; where did she go?" The White Lady asked while peeling the skin off Carla's arm. Carla let out a deep ear-piercing scream and pleaded with her to stop.

"I don't know," she yelled. "I don't know where she went."

"You're lying, you little rat. You're lying," The White Lady growled, then continued to grate her arm.

The girl lunged forward, screaming for her to stop. "She doesn't know. She's telling the truth!"

The White Lady stopped, then turned to look at the girl, her eyes ablaze. "So, you knew about this too, did you?" She let go of Carla's bloody arm and walked toward the girl, pointing the grater at her. Pieces of Carla's skin fell to the floor.

"You knew about this, and you didn't come and tell me. I'm very disappointed with you, my child. I am very disappointed indeed."

The White Lady then grabbed the girl and pulled up her shirt. She held the screaming girl down while beating her back with the grater. She didn't let go till the girl became limp in her hand, then fell to the ground, bleeding and unconscious.

23

Nassau, Bahamas, October 2018

"You found blood on the floor?"

Commissioner Maycock's brown eyes looked down at me. Standing up, he was about five inches taller than me, and he had broad shoulders. He was a big guy, almost as big as my former colleague, Mike Wagner, who had been six-foot-eight.

Thinking about him made me feel a chill go down my spine. I realized I wasn't really ready to be working again. This was supposed to be a time of vacation and relaxation. Those were Weasel's orders back home when I left.

"Promise me you'll come back rested," she had said.

The way things were going, that wasn't going to happen. I had been with the Bahamian police all day searching for the girl, and now I was telling the commissioner about my findings in the restroom and showing him the pictures of the blood on my phone.

"Yes. There were small drops of blood and scratches on the inside of the door. The door was also pulled almost off its hinges like someone had clung onto it while being dragged out. And then I found the purse in the trash can by the sink."

"And now you want me to do what?"

"Seal off the restroom. I told your officers to do it after I was in there, but they said it wasn't possible. Then they had us driving all over town and looking for Nancy Elkington when there could be valuable evidence going missing inside that restroom. It needs to be sealed off and everything secured by your crime scene techs."

The commissioner looked at me skeptically. "Because of a little blood?"

"And the scratches and the purse," I added.

Commissioner Maycock shook his head, grinning.

"What's so funny?" I asked, getting annoyed with his obvious indifference.

"Girls," he said. "They have their…you know. Blood. Sometimes it drips…on the floor."

Oh, dear God, the man is an idiot.

I felt like screaming, but held it back, trying to behave myself.

"Listen to me. You need to seal off the restroom. Something happened to Nancy Elkington in there. I see all the signs of a crime. She's an American citizen. If this reaches the mainland, you're in trouble; your tourism is in trouble. If she turns up dead on your watch, then no Americans will ever come here again. This would be the second time a young girl died here, a young American girl died here, within seven months. Even if the two deaths aren't related, you know very well how it will look to the Americans. They won't feel safe here anymore. No one listens more to fear than Americans. If you can't guarantee their safety, they won't come back. Do you understand what we're looking at here? Do you understand what is at stake? The media will gobble it up and then it's over."

I was laying it on thick, but I got the feeling that was the only language he would understand. And I could tell by the change in his expression that he was getting there.

"Yes," he simply said.

"All right. I need you to seal off that restroom before more people walk all over the evidence. Evidence we can use to solve this case and maybe make you look like you actually know what you're doing, okay?"

The commissioner nodded seriously. "Yes."

"Good."

"Tomorrow," he added.

"Excuse me?"

He looked at the clock behind me, nodding and smiling. "We will seal off the restroom tomorrow. It's five o'clock now."

I stared at him, then shook my head. Without saying anything else to him, I walked to the front desk and asked for some police tape. Then, as soon she handed me some, I left for the Straw Market where I sealed the darn door off myself.

24

NASSAU, BAHAMAS, OCTOBER 2018

Emily was lying on the bed watching Netflix on her computer when I entered the hotel room. She didn't take off her headset as I came in and sat down next to her. I leaned over and kissed her forehead. When she still didn't react, I leaned over and pressed the spacebar on the keyboard to stop the video.

"It was just getting to the good part," she moaned and looked up at me.

"Hello to you too," I said. "How was your day?"

She sat up and took off her headset. "I got some research done. Did you find the girl?"

I shook my head. "I'm afraid not."

"And what about the parents? Isn't the ship leaving tonight?" she asked.

"Yes. They got off and are staying at a hotel downtown not far from here. The two friends that they brought went back with the ship."

"Yikes. That's gotta be tough."

I exhaled. "I know. I told them to be hopeful but also prepare themselves that something had probably happened to her, that now all we can do is hope to find her alive. Seeing that look in their eyes as I said the words broke my heart. I couldn't wait to come back to you and count myself lucky that I still have you. So...what did you accomplish?"

She turned the screen so that I could see. "I found lots of stuff about Ella Maria Chauncey."

I nodded. "I didn't have much time to go through the autopsy report, but I had a few minutes this afternoon after everyone left the police station. You wanna compare notes?"

She smiled and nodded.

"You go first," I said.

"Okay, so what I know is that Ella Maria Chauncey had snuck out on the night she was killed. Her parents didn't know she was gone. She went to see her boyfriend, Henry Sakislov, whom her parents didn't want her to be with because of some dispute between the parents. The father, Henry's father, is one of the new rich Russian oligarchs and a partying playboy, the type the rest of the neighborhood doesn't care for. Nevertheless, he owns the biggest mansion in the gated community, and they even named the point after him."

"That's really good, Em," I said, very impressed. "What else have you got?"

"Henry took her boating that night with two other friends and afterward she walked home alone. According to Henry's testimony, Ella didn't want him to escort her home since she was afraid someone would see them together. He said she told him she felt safe enough to go home alone since it was a gated community. Those were the final words she said to him before she left his house. He is the last one to have seen her alive, except for the killer, of course."

I nodded. "So, he must naturally have been a main suspect, right?"

"That's what's strange," Emily said. "There are no records of him being arrested or even of him being a suspect in any of the newspapers."

"That sure is strange. You're right about that. That doesn't mean he wasn't a suspect at some point, though, just that they didn't say it in public," I said.

"Okay, my turn. According to the autopsy report, Ella Maria Chauncey was found floating in the family's pool at six o'clock the next morning by one of the maids, Sofia Rojas. The cause of death was asphyxiation, that is suffocation."

"I know what asphyxiation means," Emily said, annoyed.

"Time of death isn't very definite, but somewhere between midnight—when she left Henry's house—and six the next morning, when she was found. And there was another thing…"

I looked up, and my eyes met Emily's. She nodded to let me know she was listening.

"Her tongue was cut out."

25

Bahamas, October 2018

Nancy felt her bruises. She was still in severe pain from the beating she had received. The person hadn't shown up since, for which she was very grateful. She still didn't know how this person managed to get in and out of this strange room since she had been unconscious when the person left. Maybe it was purposefully.

Nancy sat up on the couch, touching her sore lip. Her mouth felt so dry, and she rose to her feet. There were bottles of water in a fridge leaning against the wall, and she grabbed one; she let it touch her swollen eye for a second to cool it down before she opened it and drank greedily.

I just want to go home. Will I ever see my mom and dad again? Will I ever see Billy again?

Nancy exhaled and looked around the room with her one good eye with which she could actually see. She ran a hand across the natural stone wall, seeing if there was anything indicating that there was a door somewhere when the tip of her fingers touched an edge of some sort.

Nancy stopped and looked at it more closely. Yes, there was definitely an edge there, like a crack in the wall going all the way to the ceiling. And there was one on the other side too. Nancy shrieked joyfully.

If there's a door, there's a way to open it too.

Frantically, Nancy let her fingers touch the stones on the wall, pressing them down first, then trying to pull them one after another. She had seen a wall like this before online in some video and remembered how they pressed one of the stones behind it to make it open. If only she could...if only she could...find it.

Nancy pressed and pulled each and every stone she could find and, as she reached up and pressed one a little above her head, something happened, something unexpected. There was a noise coming from inside the wall, like a clank, and then it started to move.

Nancy could hardly breathe as the door slowly slid open. She stared at it, barely able to wait for it to open properly. She could see the light coming from outside, the real light, sunlight. She was certain she could even smell the outside, the flowers and trees. She told herself that in a few seconds she would be running outside again, breathing in the fresh air, looking at the blue sky, feeling the sun on her face along with the moist Bahamian air. She couldn't wait to get off this island. As soon as she got away, she'd have to find her parents, and then they'd be going home.

Home, where Billy would be waiting for her.

Oh, Billy, I'm coming home now; I'm coming home!

But as the door opened fully and the light was revealed, something—or someone—else was too.

Nancy gasped and stepped backward. The person smiled, holding a big butcher's knife in their right hand while wearing a white apron.

"So, you found the door. I guess I should have known you would."

The person reached over and slammed a fist into her face, causing Nancy to stumble backward. The blow hit her nose so hard she heard it crack. As she lifted her head again and wiped off the blood, she saw the door slowly close and all her hope disappear with it.

"Please," she begged. "I just want to go home. Please. What do you want from me?"

The person grabbed her and forced her to the ground. Nancy then felt the cold tiles against her face and a knee in her back as she was held down. Nancy fought to get loose, but the person on top of her was heavy and strong and managed to hold her down. She couldn't see the big knife, but she knew it was there and it terrified her more than anything. What was the person's intentions with the knife? She was turned around, and they were now face to face. The person was holding the knife to her throat.

"I want your final word."

Not understanding anything, Nancy only whimpered while fighting to get loose, the blade of the knife cutting into the skin on her throat.

"Just one little word," the person said again, pressing her down. "Your final. What do you want the world to know about your final hour?"

Mostly whimpering sounds emerged from her throat, but eventually, she managed to press out something that sounded like a word, while she locked eyes with her perpetrator. The terror of seeing nothing but hatred in the eyes of the one about to kill her made her scream it.

The person then pressed a set of brutal fingers into her mouth. The fingers searched inside her for a few seconds, then grabbed her tongue and pulled it forcefully out between her lips before slicing the knife through it.

26

BAHAMAS, OCTOBER 2018

The figure watched the girl die. She squirmed on the floor, and the person made sure to keep her on her back. That way she would drown in her own blood. The person watched the blood gush out of the mouth and left the girl on the floor till she didn't move anymore, watching it all happen with great satisfaction. The person liked seeing them die and was fascinated about how different it was each time, yet how alike their bodies still acted.

But that wasn't the person's favorite part of it all. Seeing them die was one thing, and it was satisfying, yes, but the person was more in it for the chase. As soon as they were dead, the person already started thinking about finding a new one.

And it was like the demand became bigger and bigger each day.

As the girl slowly died on the floor of the person's secret room, thoughts of a new girl had already started to grow. But first, there was the matter of her final word.

The person left for a second, then came back with a bag and put it down. The person then pulled out a set of pens, needles, and ink before grabbing the girl and turning her around, undressing her, ripping her clothes off with gloved hands. The person searched the body for a perfect spot and soon found one.

Right on the lower part of the back where the skin was all soft and smooth.

27

Nassau, Bahamas, October 2018

"I just don't understand why she would confess to having killed Ella Maria Chauncey if she didn't do it," I said.

Emily nodded. "That's been my issue as well."

"And why wouldn't she talk to us when we visited her?"

"Maybe she was terrified?" Emily said, snapping her fingers. "What if someone told her to confess or they would kill her or, even better, they would kill Sydney?"

I stared at my daughter, quite surprised. "Wow. That's actually not a bad theory. You're amazing me, Em."

She smiled. "I like this. This is fun." She paused. "Not that I find murder or anything about it fun; that's not what I meant… but...doing this. With you."

I reached over and put my hand on her shoulder, feeling all kinds of mushy. It was a strange thing to be bonding over, but we were doing just that, and it made me so happy.

"I know exactly what you meant. It is not something you can easily explain to people, but I find great satisfaction in doing detective work. Why else would I be one?"

She nodded pensively. "True."

"So, what do you suggest we do next?" I asked.

She looked at the screen, then back at me. "I think we should pay that Henry dude a visit."

I chuckled. "Okay. That sounds like a very good way to go. Question that Henry *dude*. Let's do that...tomorrow. Now, I say we go down to the restaurant and get something to eat."

I stood up, but as I looked at Emily, I suddenly realized the excited look in her eyes was gone, and she was back to being that apathetic old self.

"Emily?"

She shook her head, and her eyes avoided mine. "I'll...I'll stay here."

"No, you won't. You're coming with me to the restaurant, and you'll eat. We had a deal, remember? I help Sofia, and you eat."

She shrugged. "Yeah, well, maybe it wasn't such a good idea after all."

"What are you talking about? You were just telling me how you enjoyed this? And we might end up helping one of your relatives get out of pure hell; how is that not a good idea?"

She sighed and grabbed her headphones but didn't put them on yet.

"Em, don't put those headphones on; I swear, Em, I...you promised me you'd eat, dang it."

Emily looked down at her stomach. "Yeah, well...I...don't want to."

"You don't want to...what the heck, Emily? What's going on? Where is that sweet girl I was just bonding with a few seconds ago?"

Emily answered with a shrug. I saw her glance briefly at her suitcase and walked to open the lid before she could stop me. Just as suspected, I found her scale inside of it. I grabbed it and held it out toward her.

"You brought a scale? On vacation?"

Emily looked at it, then swallowed.

"Why? Why would you bring a scale? Is that why you won't eat? Because you think you gained weight?"

"I have to keep track, okay? I can't just let go and not care like you can. I have to keep track…"

I turned around and pulled out a notebook from her suitcase as well. I flipped the pages, then felt like crying.

"You've been making graphs? This is hours…how many times do you weigh yourself during the day?"

She shrugged. "I don't know."

"Yes, you do know. It's all in here. Today you weighed yourself… every hour? Every freakin' hour, Emily? Why?"

She was about to cry, I could tell, but then she forced it away. "You wouldn't understand."

"Then explain it to me. Please, just tell me why you need to do this."

Emily looked down, then lifted the headphones.

"Don't you dare put that on, Emily; don't you dare!"

But she did. She put them on, then turned on the video and completely blocked me out. I stomped my feet angrily, grabbed the car keys and my phone, and left. I slammed the door and ran down the hall, fighting to hold back my screams.

28

NASSAU, BAHAMAS, OCTOBER 2018

I did scream. In the car. I yelled my anger out, screaming at Emily and screaming all my frustrations out while slamming my hand into the steering wheel.

The anger was soon replaced by tears. I drove away from the hotel and down by the harbor where another big cruise ship had taken over from the one that had brought Nancy Elkington and her family to the island. I wondered how many hours we had left before the story was all over the media back home. I knew the police feared that more than anything, and I was afraid they'd make some hasty arrest just to let the Americans know they had things under control. If they did, they would also close the case, and we would never find who had taken Nancy. We would never find Nancy.

I drove past the cruise ship terminals, then went up through downtown Nassau. I drove past the American Embassy then back down past Straw Market while wondering about Nancy. Where could she be? Seeing how many people walked in and out, I wondered if no one really had seen her being carried out.

Her parents had put up posters in some places, asking the public if they had *seen this girl*?

My heart sank when thinking of them. Where were they now? Still searching the streets, asking each and every person they met if they had seen their daughter, or were they sitting in their hotel room holding each other tight, worrying how to get through the night?

The thought made me accelerate past the market and continue through town, tears streaming across my cheeks. Not only for Nancy but also for Emily. Somewhere out there, Nancy was crying for someone to help her, whereas back here was Emily not wanting my help.

"I give up," I said to myself, then grabbed my phone and called Shannon.

"Hi, babe," she said.

I drove on, exhaling deeply to the sound of her voice.

"Jack? What's wrong?"

"I…I think it was a bad idea, coming here. We should never have left."

"Calm down, Jack. Tell me what's going on."

"We had the best talk, the best hour or so where we talked about the case," I said.

"The one involving Emily's relative?" she asked. "The one you told me about last night?"

"Yes. We've been working on it all day…well, something else came up for me as well, but we were talking about it, bonding so well and she was…she was almost herself, Shannon. She was just like my sweet old Emily again. We laughed and shared ideas and enjoyed each other…"

"That's great," she said. "Isn't it?"

"It was. It was more than that. It was wonderful. It made me feel so good, like I had finally had a breakthrough, but then…then I asked her if we should go eat."

"And she said no?"

"Not only that, I found a scale. In her suitcase. Along with a notebook. You should have seen it, Shannon. It was full of graphs and notes on what she ate, even if she drank a glass of water she would weigh herself. She monitored herself every hour. Every freakin' hour."

Shannon sighed. "It's getting worse."

"I...I don't know what to do. I was afraid I would say something that would hurt her, so I just left. I'm out driving now. Leaving Nassau town as we speak. I don't want to go back to her. I am so angry, Shannon, what am I to do?"

"First of all, you don't get to give up, you hear me? It is not a possibility. She's your kid. You never gave up on me, even when I had a setback a few months ago. Not when I was drinking, not when I was high on pills, you never gave up. You can't give up on her either. Second, I would say you celebrate what happened today. You did have a breakthrough, even if it was one step forward and two steps back. That's how this type of thing works, Jack. It was the same with me, remember? You and Emily experienced something together today; you bonded, and you found the old Emily. That means she is still there, Jack. And you can find her again. If you don't give up."

I sighed deeply, knowing she was right.

"Thank you," I said. "I needed to hear that."

"Glad to be able to help, honey. Now, if you'll excuse me, I need to go get Tyler. He just climbed out of bed, again. I swear he is trying to drive me nuts. I can hear his feet running around up there. Does he really think I won't hear him when he's bumping around like that? He'll never make a very good criminal."

I chuckled. "You better go get him then, before he gets himself into trouble."

"Oh, he is already in trouble," Shannon said. "Big time. Can you believe it? He stole Abigail's phone earlier today and threw it in the toilet. Good thing those phones are waterproof now, huh? But, needless to say, he's not very popular with his big sister right now."

I laughed, suddenly missing them all so terribly. I remembered Emily when she was that age and was filled with a ton of warm memories. She had always been so well-behaved, though. Never got herself into any trouble, not even when in school. She had been the sweetest little thing with her unruly curls and deep brown eyes. Gosh, I loved her.

Why did they have to grow up?

"Don't be too hard on him," I said. "He's the last one. They get extra slack, remember? That's part of the package."

"We'll see about that," Shannon said with a light laugh, then hung up. As she did, I looked at the phone while I put it down for one unforgiving second. When I looked up, I saw a young boy standing in the road, caught like a deer in my headlights.

I hit the brakes as hard as I could and turned the wheel at the same time. The car skidded sideways and slowed down, but I still hit him. The sound of my car bumping into his small body was the worst sound in the world.

29

Bahamas, July 1983

She was brought back. Less than two days after she had run away from them at the playground, Gabrielle was back at the house. The girl was lying on the mattress in her room where she had been put after the beating. She could barely move still, but as she heard the screams and yelling outside her door, she lifted her head and looked up. Seconds later, Carla unlocked the door to her room and came rushing inside.

"You have to come. They're gathering all of us in the kitchen. They need you there."

The girl lifted her gaze and looked up at Carla, who too bore visible signs of the beating she had received. The skin on her arms was swollen and frayed. The girl guessed her back looked very similar. It was very painful; that was for sure.

"I...I can't," the girl said.

"You have to," Carla said. "You know you do, come."

Carla went to her and tried to help her get up, but the girl whined in pain.

"You must," Carla said. "I don't know what she'll do to you if you're not there. Please, come."

Carla pulled her arm over her shoulder and lifted the girl up, then carried her out of the room, her face torn in deep pain as her hurting arms carried the girl into the kitchen. The girl looked at Carla's face and knew at that moment that she was forever in debt to her.

As she put her down on the floor, The White Lady fluttered inside, her dress flying in the wind behind her. She looked at each and every one of them, her nostrils flaring. Gabrielle was standing in the middle, shaking. The White Lady's son, Dylan was standing behind his mother as she faced Gabrielle.

"Have I not taken you in when you needed it the most, huh? You wanna run? You wanna get away from this place? Is that the way you show gratefulness for everything I have done for you? You're illegal, my dear. You're in this country illegally. No one cares what happens to you. If you're arrested, you'll be thrown in jail. Do you know what jail is like in this place? Well, it's a lot worse than here, I can tell you that much. And once they put you in there, they'll forget about you. You'll rot in that hellhole. I saved you from that fate when I picked you up at the harbor. I took care of you. I have given you a roof over your head; I make sure you eat, that you have a bed to sleep in. And this is how you repay me? You want to have freedom? You have no rights. People who come here illegally have no rights at all. If you don't behave, if you don't obey me, then I see no other solution than to call for an immigration officer. And do you know what he will do to you? You'll be lucky if he only throws you in jail and loses the key. He might as well kill you and bury you outside of town in a field with all the other illegal aliens. I am really saving you here. I am helping you out."

The White Lady snorted and looked at all of them.

"That goes for all of you in here. There is nowhere you can run. This is your home now."

Gabrielle started to cry, holding a hand to her face. The White Lady gave her a disgusted look.

"Get down on your knees," she said.

Gabrielle answered with another sob.

"Get down on your knees, I said," The White Lady repeated. "I want you to beg for forgiveness."

Gabrielle sobbed again, then looked up at the woman in front of her.

"On your knees!"

The White Lady clenched her fist. Sobbing deeply, Gabrielle fell to her knees.

"I'm sorry," she said. "I am so sorry!"

The White Lady snorted and looked down at the weeping Gabrielle. It wasn't until now that the girl noticed Gabrielle had bruises all over and that her nose was bleeding.

The White Lady looked at two of the women standing behind Gabrielle, their heads bent.

"Take her to the shed," she said.

"NO!" Gabrielle wailed and threw herself on the tiles. "Please, no!"

30

Nassau, Bahamas, October 2018

It was my luck that I wasn't going very fast. As soon as the car came to a halt, I jumped out and ran to the boy lying in the street. My heart was pounding in my chest as I prayed to God that he wasn't dead.

Please let him be all right.

When I saw that he was moving and heard him moan, I felt a wave of relief rush through my body. I knelt next to him as he lay on the side of the road.

"Are you okay, kid?"

The boy looked at me. I scanned his body quickly for any blood gushing out, in case an artery had burst somewhere or if he had been badly hurt somehow but found none. A few scrapes on his arms were bleeding, but that was all.

"Can you sit up?" I asked.

He nodded, then rose his torso to an upright position. He felt his side, and I realized that was where I had hit him. Probably bruised a few ribs, maybe even broke them. The boy lifted his shirt, and he had a bad bruise there. I grimaced, my stomach in a thousand knots.

"I am so, so sorry," I said and helped him up on his feet. "I am so sorry. I feel awful."

"I'm okay," the boy said with a strained look to his face.

"No, let me take you to the hospital," I said. "We need to make sure nothing is broken. You could have some bleeding in places we can't see. I don't want to risk..."

The boy shook his head. "No. No hospital."

"No hospital? But...you really should go...You took quite the blow there; there's no telling what might have been damaged..."

He shook his head again.

"No."

I sighed, then looked behind him as I spotted a flock of birds, black vultures circling the bushy area behind him. Their presence had my attention immediately, and I felt a chill go down my spine.

Something dead was in there behind those bushes.

Was that why the boy was running? Did he see something?

I turned to ask him for answers but found nothing but the empty road behind me. I checked my surroundings a few times to see if I could find him, but he was gone.

Dang it.

Curious to see what the birds were so interested in, I pressed through the thick bushes and, as I walked closer, I realized the stench of death was all around me. In this heat, the smell was overwhelming and almost suffocating. I stopped when I reached water and wild growing mangrove. Lying beneath the mangroves, stuck in the roots, was the body of a young woman. She was naked and looked peaceful as she lay there in the mushy water. It was hard to recognize her features in the bruised and swollen face, but the long blonde hair floating in the water gave her identity away.

It had to be Nancy Elkington.

31

Nassau, Bahamas, October 2018

"You say he just took off? I don't understand."

Commissioner Maycock gave me a look. It was the third time he had asked about the boy, and he was beginning to sound like he didn't quite believe he even existed.

"Yes," I said and looked in the direction I had last seen the boy. We were standing on the side of the road. They had blocked the area off while searching it and securing the body from the water. "I ran into him with my car, and I told him I would take him to the hospital, but he didn't want to go."

"Have you been drinking?" Maycock asked.

I sighed. "No, for the fourth time, I didn't drink anything. I was upset because I had a fight with my daughter. Listen, I am tired, can I please go back now?"

"So you can leave the country?" he asked.

Now it was my turn to give the man a puzzled look. "You're accusing me of something here?"

"How did you know the body was in there?" Maycock asked, not answering my question.

I felt like screaming but held it back. "I told you. There was a boy..."

"And that boy conveniently just vanished into thin air," Maycock interrupted me.

"You're kidding me. You think I'm lying?"

"I think you have a very good cover, Mr. Ryder, being a detective on vacation, and I also think you're very clever."

I sighed and rubbed my forehead. "There was a boy. I am not making this up."

"Americans like to come here and cause lots of trouble, thinking they can get away with it. The fact is, Mr. Ryder, we don't know anything about you, do we? We don't know why you are really here. We allowed you to read the autopsy, and you got ideas, didn't you? To cut out her tongue the way someone did to Miss Ella Maria Chauncey, am I right?"

This is a freaking joke; this man is a joke!

I exhaled. "Are you charging me with anything? Otherwise, I would like to go now. My daughter is alone back at the hotel."

"If you even have a daughter," he said.

"Am I under arrest?" I asked.

"Not yet," Maycock said. "But don't leave the island."

"You know where to find me," I said and left with an annoyed moan.

I got into my car and drove back toward the hotel. I had called Emily and told her what happened and that I was going to be back late, but I had never imagined it would be past midnight before I got back to her. I rushed into town and drove through the now-empty small streets, wondering about Nancy Elkington and her poor parents. I couldn't stop thinking about what Maycock had told me.

Nancy had her tongue cut out just like Ella Maria Chauncey. It had to be the same killer, didn't it? And that meant Emily was right. Sofia was innocent. I hadn't fully believed it earlier, but now I did.

32

Lyford Cay, Bahamas, October 2018

Henry Sakislov greeted us in the hallway of his enormous mansion. I thought I had seen it all when visiting the Chauncey's, but this was extreme. It was too much for my taste.

I had called that morning, asking to meet with him, telling him I was investigating the killing of Ella Maria Chauncey. I hadn't expected him to, but he had agreed to see me. I had also told him to bring his father, but he was out of town.

Henry was a real looker and had one of those smiles that made the girls fall for him instantaneously. Emily was no different. When he shook her hand, I noticed the nervous tic around her mouth as she tried to smile. I knew her well enough to know that she thought he was cute.

We sat in the living room, and a woman served us coffee. I knew most Bahamians either worked in the tourist industry taking care of wealthy American tourists or worked for the wealthy Americans who chose to live on the islands, taking care of their every need, whether it was gardening or housekeeping. I didn't like how it sort of reminded me of colonialism, and I especially didn't like for Emily to experience this. I had always made a big deal of her being equal to the rest of us, even though it was hard for her never to experience racism even in Florida. It hadn't happened much in school, but it was the little things. Like how all the black kids sat together at lunch or the teacher only calling on her for easy questions. It didn't take her long to realize she was different, and that broke my heart. Now, I feared she would see it again being in a place where there was a pronounced difference between races.

"Thank you so much," I said to the woman who served us the coffee, trying hard to make sure that she knew I appreciated her and noticed her. The woman nodded shyly. As she put down the bowl of chocolates, I noticed she winced like she was in pain. I looked at her wrist and noticed it was badly bruised.

"How did you get that?" I asked.

She retracted and hid her wrist.

"She fell," Henry said.

I turned and looked at him, wondering why he felt compelled to answer for her.

"Yesterday," he continued. "On the stairs. I wanted to take her to the ER, but she wouldn't hear of it. Most of the Bahamians don't have insurance and can't afford to get treatment. I even told her I would pay for it, but she wouldn't have it. Proud people, the Bahamians."

The woman gave me another shy look, then nodded politely and left. I kept looking after her as she disappeared, her head bowed.

"So, you wanted to talk about Ella Maria?" Henry asked, and I turned to face him, then nodded.

"Yes, Emily here is related to Sofia Rojas and her daughter Sydney," I said. As I mentioned Sydney's name, Henry blushed, then almost choked on his coffee. He coughed a few times, then forced a smile.

"Oh, really?"

"Yes, and to cut to the chase, we believe Sofia is innocent."

Henry coughed again. "Oh, really? Why so?"

I leaned forward and looked into the young boy's eyes. "Because the killer just struck again."

33

LYFORD CAY, BAHAMAS, OCTOBER 2018

"Is that so?"

I was observing Henry as he put the coffee cup down. It wasn't even shaking in his hands. Yet I sensed something was off. He was just good at hiding it.

"A young girl named Nancy Elkington visiting from a cruise ship was taken a few days ago, and she turned up last night in the water, killed."

"And just how is that related to what happened to Ella Maria?" he asked.

"Her tongue was cut out."

Henry nodded. "I see."

I leaned back in the chair I was sitting in and sipped from my coffee cup while watching the boy. He didn't seem shocked, but he didn't seem indifferent either. He was very hard to read.

"And just how might I be able to help?" he asked, sounding very polite and genuine, yet detached.

"I would like to know more about Ella Maria, and your relationship with the family," I asked.

"I see. Well, it has never been good between our families, as you might know."

"So I have heard, yes," I said.

"Ella's parents didn't want us to see one another because of the feud. But we were young and in love and well...you know. Forbidding us to see one another just makes it that much more interesting, right?"

"So, you saw each other anyway?" I asked.

"Of course. Our parents travel a lot and well...they are quite busy with their own lives, and so...it wasn't exactly hard for us. Ella was wild and liked to do things her family didn't approve of."

"For instance?"

He shrugged. "Just stuff like going boating and scuba diving at night, drinking, and so on."

"Why do you think that was? Why do you think she was so wild?" I asked. Henry kept staring at Emily, and I didn't like the look in his eyes. I regretted bringing her.

He chortled. "Isn't it obvious? They kept her on a tight leash all her life, never let her do anything. You can't do that to a girl like Ella. Or to any girl. At some point, young girls want to fly."

"And so, you helped her do that?" I said.

He chuckled. "Ella didn't need any help. She managed fine by herself."

I nodded. "I see."

"And the feud between your families, what was that about?"

Henry snorted. "It really isn't that interesting. It's a typical feud in wealthy communities like these. We're the newly rich, and we're annoying them, the old rich, because we change things up and do it differently than what they're used to. They have boring stuck up lives. We like to have fun. And when we moved here, my dad bought up a lot of land and built a house bigger than any of theirs."

"So, you say they're jealous?"

"You said that; I didn't," he said and sipped his coffee again, smiling endearingly at Emily. "It's all very ridiculous if you ask me. But us kids can't really do anything about it except laugh at them."

I wrote a couple of notes on my pad, then looked up at him

again. "How did the Chaunceys react when they found the body of their daughter?"

"What do you mean?" he asked.

"You were the last one to see her alive. Did they, at any point, blame you for it?" I asked.

Henry chuckled again and nodded. "They sure did. I wasn't even allowed to go to the funeral. Everyone believed it was me."

"Everyone? But you were never arrested?"

Henry thought for a second. "Well, no, but that doesn't mean people don't think you did something. I think a lot of them still think I did it. The school won't even let me come back, and it's been seven months. They're afraid that me being there will cause too much trouble, they say. So, my dad hired private teachers for me. I don't mind; I didn't like the school anyway. But the hatred between our families is worse than ever. I'm sure the Chaunceys still blame me. If not for killing her directly then for luring her out at nighttime or not walking her home properly."

I rubbed my chin while staring at the young boy, wondering if the police had simply just arrested Sofia to secure peace, to make the rich white people feel safe again, to make sure they didn't leave the island? They didn't dare touch the wealthy white Americans, did they? Of course not. Not even when everyone else thought he had done it. And so, they had thrown themselves at Sofia like wolves on prey. The question was, had she done anything besides find the body floating in the family's pool? Was that the sole reason she was imprisoned? If so, then I was her only hope, and there was no way I was going to simply look the other way.

"So, did you do it?" I asked, not because I believed he would say yes, but to see his reaction and to at least have asked.

He shook his head, not seeming surprised by my question.

"No."

"Do you have any idea who might have wanted to hurt her?" I asked.

He shook his head a second time, but I saw something in his eyes that told me he wasn't being completely honest with me.

I got up and reached out my hand. "Thank you for your time," I said as he took it. "I would like to talk to your father at some point; when will he be home?"

An expression of hopelessness emerged on Henry's face.

"I don't know," he said. "He never really tells me where he goes and when he's coming home."

I nodded and handed him my card. "Just tell him to give me a call when he gets back, okay?"

Henry nodded, but I wasn't convinced he was actually going to do it.

"Sure."

34

BAHAMAS, JULY 1983

The girl had heard about the shed but never known exactly what it was. Not till Gabrielle was put inside of it did she know.

It was a small metal garden shed in the part of the yard that no one used, which was covered by the tall palm trees and dense bushes. Gabrielle was placed in there and the door padlocked from the outside.

The first day that Gabrielle spent in there, the girl didn't dare to go out there, fearing The White Lady would see her and maybe punish her. But as she woke up the next morning and Carla opened her door, she rushed out there before The White Lady woke up.

At first, she didn't dare to go close and stood far away from the shed, staring at it. She could hear Gabrielle knocking on the metal door and it made the hairs stand up on the back of her neck, even though it was so hot out that she could barely breathe.

How was Gabrielle breathing in there if she could barely breathe out here? She wondered and took a few steps closer. Gabrielle was still knocking, calling for help, and the girl walked so close she could place a hand on the shed, but she had to pull it back fast because the metal was so hot it burned her hand.

She sat in the grass while staring at the shed and listening to Gabrielle knocking and crying for help for about an hour before Carla came out to get the girl and pull her back inside. She took her into the kitchen, then knelt in front of her, brushing off the grass from her clothes.

"You can't go out there," she said.

"Why can't we let her out?" the girl asked.

"She's being punished for what she did," Carla said. "It's her own fault. Just be glad it's not you in there."

"But it's hot," the girl said. "The metal is burning hot."

Carla shushed her, then told her to go peel the potatoes and forget everything about it. But she couldn't. It was all the girl could think about all day long as she went about her day, taking care of Dylan, listening in on his private lessons, and washing the sheets that Carla told her to. But she couldn't concentrate on any of her chores. All she could think about was Gabrielle and, as she did the laundry, she could still hear her screaming. The sounds of her terrifying cries were haunting her.

Later in the evening when it had gone dark outside, she took the chance and ran into the yard, only to realize that the screaming and knocking had stopped. Heart throbbing in her throat, the girl sat in the grass and stared at the shed in front of her. She heard a noise that, at first, she thought was rats, but soon she realized came from inside the shed. It was a scraping sound, sounding just like when the rats went through the garbage in the big containers in the back. She would often hear them when taking out the trash and she hated it more than any sound in the world.

As the scraping slowly died out too, she realized she now hated the sound of silence more than that. The girl stared at the shed, then put a hand to it again and scraped on it, wanting to let Gabrielle know she was out there. But there was no answer, no sound coming from inside of it. Crying desperately, the girl then knocked on the shed, hoping Gabrielle would knock back, but she remained silent.

Eyes filled to the brim with tears, the girl then turned around and ran back inside the house, running as fast as she could without falling, praying she would be able to outrun Gabrielle's ghost that she was certain would come back to haunt her.

And it did. For years to come, the scraping sound of Gabrielle's nails clawing on the metal door would keep her awake at night, causing her to scream her terror out.

35

Nassau, Bahamas, October 2018

"What do you make of him?" I asked, looking at Emily. We had stopped to get some lunch on the way back from Lyford Cay and brought it back to the hotel. Emily had ordered a salad with chicken and was eating it, actually enjoying it, if I wasn't much mistaken. I didn't say anything but just watched her eat. Meanwhile, I had a jerked mahi-mahi sandwich that was out of this world.

"He's definitely lying about something," she said.

"Do you think he killed her?" I asked.

Emily exhaled pensively. "That's a hard one. He's very slick. A real womanizer."

I chuckled hearing her say that word since it was so old-fashioned. "I thought you young people said player," I said.

She shrugged, not really caring that I was mocking her. She was so deeply into solving this case; I felt proud of her. It had been years since I had seen her care this much about anything, to be honest.

"But is he a killer?" she asked, pointing at me with her fork.

"That's the question, Miss Marple," I said.

She wrinkled her nose. "Who?"

"Never mind," I said, shaking my head with a grin.

"But we do agree it's the same killer in both cases, right?" Emily asked.

I nodded. "It has to be. At least I think so. The Royal Bahamian Police don't, but I think we could prove them wrong. I mean cutting their tongues out sure sounds like a signature from a serial killer. I just wished I knew what else was similar in the two cases. I mean, they were both found in water as well, but what else?"

"Can't we get to the autopsy report?" Emily asked.

I shrugged. "I don't think the police here will be very cooperative, especially not since they see me as a main suspect."

"They do what?" Emily asked.

I shook my head. "It's nothing but a misunderstanding. I found the body, so they apparently think I might have placed it there too. I have a feeling it's a thing here. That the commissioner, that Maycock guy, he believes a lot in whoever finds the body must be a suspect. I mean he did it to Sofia and now me."

Emily chuckled. "He probably read it in some book."

"Or saw it on some American crime show, is more likely. I don't think he reads many books, to be honest."

That made Emily laugh. I smiled when hearing her light laughter. It felt good to be with her like this again. This was the Emily I knew and loved. And us bonding like this over the case seemed to be the thing that brought her back out. It was like she completely forgot to be anorexic.

"But isn't there some other way to get ahold of an autopsy report?" Emily asked. "Will they write about it in the papers?"

"They'll only write whatever the commissioner tells them, and I have a feeling he might leave out everything that will make it look like this is the same killer since it will only create chaos and panic, and that's bad for tourism."

"Not to mention the fact that he'll come out as looking pretty silly for having arrested Sofia for the first murder," Emily said and finished her salad. She put her silverware down on the plate, and I tried hard to hide my joy over the fact that she had finished it all. It wasn't much, but it was a small victory.

"So, these autopsy reports," she said pensively. "Are they electronic?"

"Sure," I said. "The copy they gave me was printed by his secretary from her old stationary computer. Why?"

Emily nodded.

"I might have an idea."

36

Nassau, Bahamas, October 2018

I went to bed while Emily was still on her laptop. She wouldn't let me in on what she was up to, so I watched TV until I dozed off and finally decided to go to bed. A few hours later, I woke up as the light from her screen lit up the room. I rubbed my eyes and sat up.

"Emily?"

She didn't answer. She was staring at the screen, her fingers dancing across the keyboard, her eyes fixated on what was on the screen, looking like she was almost hypnotized by it.

"What time is it?" I asked and looked at the clock underneath the TV. "It's three a.m.! Why are you still up, Em? Em?"

She paid no attention to me but continued whatever she was doing. I got out of bed and walked to her.

"Emily, baby. You really should get some sleep. It's not health…"

She stopped me, holding a finger in the air. "I'm almost done."

I sat down next to her on the bed. "What are you doing?"

She turned her head to face me. "I just gained us access to Nancy Elkington's police report."

Emily turned the laptop so that I could see. My eyes grew wide in the darkness, and I was suddenly very much awake. My eyes stared at the screen and the report in front of me, then at Emily.

"Em, I am…I am in…when did you learn how to do something like this?" I asked.

She shrugged. "I've had a lot of time on my hands lately."

"So, this is what you've been up to in that room of yours? Hacking? That's what you're doing now?"

"Please, don't be mad," she said.

"It's illegal, Emily. Have you been…hacking from your room, from our house at home?"

"Just a little bit."

"You can't break the law just a little bit, Em," I said with a deep exhale. "You either do it, or you don't."

"But I am always careful," she said. "I know how to reroute the IP address, so no one can trace me. I am still a newbie, but I'm actually getting pretty good at it."

"Well, of course you are," I replied. "You're good at anything you set your mind to. That doesn't make it less illegal."

"Please, don't be mad."

I stared at her, my eyes softening slowly. "I can never be mad at you. At least not for very long. You know that."

She smiled and pushed the computer closer to me so that we could both see the screen.

"Besides, this might end up helping someone. It's not all bad," she said. "We'll just take a quick look, then get out."

I chuckled and leaned closer. "Just one look, then."

"It looks like they're not done with the medical examiner's report yet," she said, "but there are some preliminary examinations in the file. You were right; the tongue had been cut out. They don't know the cause of death yet or the time."

"There are photos," I said. "Can you open them, please?"

"Sure," she said and clicked on one of them. It showed Nancy Elkington right after she had been dragged out of the water, where I had found her. The sight of Nancy Elkington's naked bruised body made Emily wince, but her reaction wasn't as brutal as I had feared. She seemed to look at it with the eyes of someone looking for clues, as opposed to someone she could have known. Emily's response had a very nice distance to it, a professionalism that surprised me in such a young girl.

"Can you zoom in on the picture right there?" I said and pointed to a photo that was taken of the girl's back. I pointed at a mark on the lower part of her back. "Right there."

"Sure," she said and zoomed in. "What is that? A tattoo?"

I nodded. "Yes, but look at how swollen it is."

"Is that because it's been in the water?" she asked.

"Maybe," I said. "Or it could be because it is very fresh."

"What does it say?" she asked and zoomed even closer. The picture became pixelated, but I could still read it just fine.

"Can you take a screenshot of that for me please?"

Emily gave me a look.

"What do you think it means?"

I shook my head and wrote the word down on my notepad. "I don't know…yet."

PART III

37

Bahamas, October 2018

The itch was back. The person didn't really understand how it could be back so fast. It should have stayed away for at least a couple of weeks or at least days. But there it was, and it wouldn't stop. The person knew there was no way out of it.

There needed to be another one.

The person had about an hour to kill, so there was time to check her out. The person knew exactly which girl should be next and where to find her. The person had kept an eye on her for quite some time and knew she would be perfect. The person had held back, kept her as a treat for one special day, waited for the perfect timing.

And that was now.

The person walked up to the clubhouse and entered from the poolside, smiling at a woman walking out with her small dog in her purse. The young girl was waiting tables, smiling at a couple to whom she had just served cocktails. Smiling for those great tips she would soon get, and she got a lot of them. The person had been observing her for quite some time and had seen how she almost shoveled them in. Especially the men liked her, which was no surprise. She was a gorgeous girl, small and blonde with a slim waist. She looked very much like the girl the person had just gotten rid of.

The figure watched the girl as she worked the floor and while listening in on her casual conversations with the customers or with the other waiters. The eavesdropping over the past several months had given the person lots of important information on the girl. Now, the person didn't like to know their names, since their names were of no importance, but couldn't avoid seeing the name tag reading Coraline. The person also knew that Coraline was nineteen and that she was in the Bahamas taking a year off before starting college back in Boston next year. She had no boyfriend since she wanted to make the most of this year and not let some guy hold her back, as she explained to the receptionist one day. Her parents were divorced, an ugly one, and she had lived with her father all her life, going through several stepmoms who all wanted him for his money and all wanted her out of their way. Coraline was wealthy, and her father had gotten her the job at the clubhouse in one of the most lucrative neighborhoods in the world. She knew he had gotten her that because he thought it was a safe place to send her now that she absolutely wanted to go into the world and *meet people* like most young people did. And probably also because he assumed she would meet some nice guy there, some rich guy or someone who was a son of just that, someone who could provide for her for the rest of her life, or at least till they got divorced and she ran with half of what he had. Coraline's dad was rich, but not overwhelmingly wealthy the way most people living in Lyford Cay were. The person guessed he saw an opportunity to make sure his daughter was taken care of by getting her this job. It wasn't a wrong assumption.

Looking at it from the outside, Lyford Cay would seem like a very safe place to send your precious daughter.

38

Nassau, Bahamas, October 2018

Mrs. Elkington looked like she had aged ten years since I last saw her. She was pale, almost ash-grey and her eyes completely void of any life. Her husband was standing by the window, looking out, his arms crossed behind his back. He hadn't uttered a word since I entered.

"Have you been sleeping at all?" I asked them.

I was visiting them at the hotel where they were staying. Emily was with me and had sat down on a couch in the back.

Mrs. Elkington shook her head. Her eyes were swollen from crying. "I…I don't know how to…there are all the arrangements, we need to get her a proper burial, you know? And…they won't…they don't know when they'll be able to release the body to us."

"They need it for the investigation," I said and placed a hand on top of Mrs. Elkingtons. "They haven't done the autopsy yet, and it might take a few days, maybe even a week or more. I don't know how fast they work around here, but back home…"

I didn't get to finish the sentence before Mrs. Elkington burst into tears. Emily sprang to her feet and handed her a tissue box from the bathroom. She pulled one out and wiped her eyes. There were no traces of make-up on the tissue when she was done. Even if she had put any on this morning, she had been crying so much it was already gone.

"I am so sorry," she said. "It overwhelms me from time to time."

"It's only natural," I said and glanced at Mr. Elkington. It wasn't the ones who cried I usually worried about the most. It was the ones who bottled it all up.

"He's been staring out that window ever since we received the news," she said, leaning forward and talking in a low voice like he wasn't able to hear her. "I can't get him to eat anything, and he doesn't say a word. Just stares and stares out that stupid window."

I smiled, realizing all Mrs. Elkington needed was for him to be with her in this, her hour of need. For him to hold her hand and talk to her. But that wasn't always the way people reacted.

"He'll come along. We all grieve differently."

She exhaled. "She was our only daughter, you know? We had her late. Thought I couldn't conceive since it didn't happen for years and then suddenly, puff, there she was. She was such a sweetheart, so loving and so…did you know she won an essay contest when she was only in fifth grade? She wanted to be a writer." She glared at her husband. "He was so proud of her. Prouder than any father could possibly be."

"I bet," I said and glanced at Emily. I hoped she knew just how proud I was of her. It tormented me that she couldn't love herself, that she couldn't see how amazing she really was. I guess Mrs. Elkington now wondered if their daughter ever knew how proud they were of her. They would never get the chance to tell her again.

"How are they doing on the investigation?" Mrs. Elkington said. "Are they any closer to finding out who did this…awful thing to my daughter?"

I exhaled. Getting closure was so important for the relatives at this point, but it was rarely something I could provide this early. I knew they expected me to take part in the investigation, which I was in a way, but not in the way they assumed I was. I had tried to reach out to Commissioner Maycock, but he had told me they had it all under control and that they would let the Americans know once they had news. I didn't know if by Americans he meant me or Nancy's parents or maybe the Embassy, but I assumed he didn't want me snooping around and finding fault in his investigation. He wanted to do this his way and, by acting like he believed I had something to do with it, he could keep me as far away as he wanted to.

"I know that they are working very hard," I said. "It is their top priority right now and..."

Mr. Elkington made a sound that was more like a snort, and I stopped talking.

"Don't mind him," his wife said. "He's just angry at them for not taking it serious enough when she went missing. That's not your fault, Detective Ryder. You did the best you could. I know you did."

"And rest assured I will keep a close eye on this case and let you know if anything new happens. But right now, I have a question I need to ask you both."

I pulled out my phone and found the screenshot that Emily had taken for me and sent me. I showed it to Mrs. Elkington.

"Did Nancy have a tattoo?" I asked.

Mrs. Elkington looked at the photo, then back up at me. She glanced briefly at her husband.

"John, come see this."

He grunted something, then decided to come anyway and looked at it over her shoulder.

"I have never seen this before," he said.

"So, you have never seen this tattoo before?" I said, feeling a small pinch of hope grow inside of me.

"No," Mrs. Elkington said sounding appalled. "We would certainly know if our daughter had something like that on her body, destroying it in that way that the young do today."

"And she couldn't have been hiding it from you?"

"We would have seen it," Mrs. Elkington said. "On the cruise ship at the pool. We saw her in her bikini every day. Plus, she would never do that to us. She knew we were very much against tattoos."

"So, it is new," I concluded. "Could she have gotten it before she was kidnapped?"

Mrs. Elkington shrugged. "I don't think she would ever do that to us, but it is, of course, a possibility. I could try and ask Maria, the friend she was with when they left the ship. Wait a sec," she said and got up.

Mrs. Elkington walked to her purse and pulled out a phone, then left us with it against her ear.

I could hear her talking in the hallway for a few minutes before she returned, shaking her head.

"No, they didn't get any tattoos. Maria said it wasn't something Nancy would ever do. She didn't like tattoos and was too afraid of needles even to consider it."

"And what about what it says?" I asked. "Does that mean anything to you?"

Mrs. Elkington looked at the picture closely again, then shook her head. "*Joy*? What is that even supposed to mean?"

39

Lyford Cay, Bahamas, October 2018

Coraline Stuart was just finishing work. She went to the lockers in the back and found her clothes, then started to get undressed, then changed back into her own clothes.

Working at Lyford Cay was fun and a great work environment. Not that Coraline had anything to compare it with since it was her first and only job ever. But she liked it; she liked getting by on her own for once and making money. Coraline wasn't used to being on her feet this much all day, so she sat down and massaged them, just as another waiter, Meghan, came in.

"So, what are you up to tonight?" she asked. "You have the day off tomorrow, don't you?"

Coraline smiled and nodded.

"Don't tell me you're seeing *him* again?" Meghan said, giving her a look of concern.

"Why not?" Coraline chuckled.

"Oh, you are in deep waters there, missy. He is trouble; you know that, right?" she asked.

Coraline groaned. "I'm just having fun. That's all."

"Promise me you're not putting more into it than that. And even so, having fun can be dangerous."

Coraline rolled her eyes at her friend while putting on her sandals, the ones that went so well with her yellow summer dress. "You're starting to sound a lot like my dad."

Meghan shrugged. "So, where is he taking you?"

"He said he'd pick me up in his car when I got off."

Meghan slammed her locker shut, then gave Coraline a look. "Well, have fun, but be careful, promise?"

"Of course."

Meghan left, and Coraline looked at her face in the mirror. She found her make-up bag and started to apply some mascara and eyeliner. She went a little too heavy on the eyeliner and had to remove some of it using a Q-Tip. She bent her head down to wet it under the faucet, then looked up into the mirror again. When her eyes were raised, she spotted someone standing behind her, a face staring at her over her shoulder.

"Oh, dear Lord, you scared me," she said, holding a hand to her chest. She reapplied the eyeliner while the person stared at her, head slightly tilted, eyes scrutinizing her. Coraline looked at her reflection again, then smacked her lips.

"How do I look?" she said, glancing at the person in the mirror behind her. The person came closer and stood right behind her, and she could feel the person's breath on her neck.

"Beautiful," the person said.

Coraline smiled from ear to ear. "I do, don't I?"

"You really do," the person replied.

Coraline made a few kissing faces at herself, then turned to face the person standing behind her, when she felt a sharp prick of a needle biting into her thigh.

40

Nassau, Bahamas, October 2018

We ate dinner at the hotel's restaurant, sitting by the pool, surviving through yet another of their famous karaoke nights. I had conch fries—again—and Emily stuck with a salad. Something was very different about the way she approached her food. She didn't push it around on the plate twenty-four times before eating any of it; she didn't arrange it differently like she usually did, probably to make it look like she ate. No, during this meal, she simply sat down and started to eat while her mind seemed to be elsewhere. I gobbled down my conch fries and coconut shrimp and I watched her closely, wondering what was going on in that beautiful head of hers.

I drank from my local beer, Kalik, which was very refreshing in the heat, listening to some guy sing an Adele song completely out of tune. I couldn't even decipher which song it was.

"I bet he has done it before," Emily said through the loud music, pointing at me with her fork.

"Why do you say that?" I asked, biting down on yet another conch fry, crunching loudly.

"Well, we agree he killed Ella Maria too, right? Why should it have started there?" she asked.

I nodded, smiling. I had had the very same thought during the day.

"What if the local authorities simply didn't make the connections?" she continued. "Either because they didn't want to because having a serial killer on the loose is bad for tourism, or because they're not qualified enough to see it, or even look for it."

"Qualified," I repeated laughing. "You're being very diplomatic. I would have used another word, but yours is better."

She ignored me, too deep into her thoughts.

"I'm serious here. A guy like him could have gotten away with this for years without getting caught."

"That is very likely," I said and grabbed the last fry. I had spoken to Shannon earlier, and both she and the kids were doing well. Tyler had flushed Abigail's favorite *Monster High* doll in the toilet, and she had responded by pulling the leg off of Tyler's favorite teddy bear. But other than that, they were fine, Shannon had promised me. She had sewn the leg back onto the bear and Tyler had said he was sorry for trying to take her doll for a swim. I knew it had to be tough for Shannon, and I felt for her, I really did.

Emily rose to her feet.

"Where are you going?" I asked.

"I'm done," she said.

I looked at her plate; she had only eaten half of her salad. It disappointed me, but there was something different with the way she refused to eat this time. It didn't seem like it was because she wanted to lose weight or was even focused on that. There was something else. Something urgent on her heart.

"Well, I'm not," I said and threw out my arms. "I still have my shrimp and half of my beer left."

She didn't even look at me. She just grabbed the keycard and started to walk.

"I'll see you up there."

41

Bahamas, July 1983

They carried her body away. The girl watched as they opened the door to the shed and Gabrielle's lifeless body slid out. Her skin was swollen and covered in blisters. The White Lady took one disgusted look at her, then told the girls to *get rid of it.*

So, they did. Crying and sobbing heavily, Carla grabbed Gabrielle's limp body and, with the help from two other girls, they carried her into the backyard, where the gardener dug a deep hole for them to put her in.

Carla sang a couple of songs, and they cried together, while the girl watched them from a distance, feeling the metallic taste of anger rise in the back of her mouth, tasting like bile.

When they were done, Carla approached the girl, reached out her hand, and the girl took it. They walked in silence back to the kitchen where they continued their chores.

The girl watched Carla as she cried into the flour while baking. She looked up at her, then asked.

"How come the police don't come?"

Carla shook her head in answer.

"How come they don't arrest The White Lady?" the girl continued.

Carla sniffled. "The police don't care about us."

"Why not?" the girl asked, feeling tears of anger pile up.

"Because we're illegal," Carla said. "We're not allowed to be here."

"B-but she's dead. Gabrielle was killed. The White Lady killed her," the girl said, clenching her jaw.

Carla exhaled. She had her fingers deeply planted inside the dough, and her scarred arms were covered in flour.

"She broke the rules. She ran away and so she was punished. If the police had gotten to her, she would have been killed too. We told her it was too dangerous, and she wouldn't listen. She brought this upon herself, upon us as well."

"But..."

Carla pulled her hands out of the dough, then cleaned them before grabbing the girl by the shoulders. She forced her to look into her eyes.

"You have to let it go, you hear me? All we can do is move on. You are lucky. The White Lady adores you. If you treat her well and follow her rules, then one day you might get a lot of freedom. Like me. She trusts me, which means I get to leave the house from time to time. I get to go into town and run errands. I get to go places because she knows I will always come back. If you behave well, if you show her she can trust you, then one day you might get that too. You might get to have the freedom that I have. A girl like Gabrielle didn't understand that. But you do. I see it in your eyes. The White Lady cares for us. She takes good care of us. We have nowhere else to go."

The girl stared into Carla's eyes and knew at this moment that she loved her. Carla had been like a mother to her through all her life in the house. She was the closest she got to having a parent.

"Do you understand what I am saying?" Carla said. "There are other ways of surviving. Running away is not one of them. You can get plenty of freedom if you just play by the rules, if you play your cards right. Are you listening?"

The girl bit her lip, then nodded.

"Y-yes."

Carla then pulled her into a warm embrace and kissed the top of her head.

"Smart girl."

42

Nassau, Bahamas, October 2018

I finished my beer and my shrimp, then walked back up to the hotel room where I found Emily at her computer. She was staring like she was hypnotized by the screen, not even noticing that I had entered.

I turned on the TV, then flipped through a few channels till I felt overwhelmed by my exhaustion and dozed off.

When I woke up a few hours later, the TV was still on, and Emily was still awake.

"Are you never going to sleep again?" I asked and turned off the TV. My eyes felt like I had sand in them.

She looked up and smiled. "I can sleep when I get older…like you."

"Ha-ha. Very funny," I said and sat on her bed. "But I am serious, Em. Staying up night after night isn't healthy."

She looked at me. I saw a spark in her eyes I hadn't seen in a very long time. It overwhelmed me with joy.

"I found something," she said.

I blinked a few times to see better. "What's that?"

"Three cases," she said.

I was suddenly fully awake. "Three?"

She nodded. "Look."

She moved the laptop so that I could better see what she had been working on.

"I didn't even have to hack," she said, smiling. "Nothing illegal. I just found the stories in old online newspapers."

"Details, please," I said.

Emily sent me a smile. "First case I found was from 2010. A young girl, Laurie Roberts, age twenty-four, was found floating in a pond. She was white just like Ella and Nancy, and...her tongue was cut out."

"And tattoos?"

"The articles don't say anything about tattoos. We'll need to get to the autopsy report to find that out."

"Okay, and what about her origins? Where did she come from?"

"She was American," Emily said. "From California. She was backpacking with a friend when she disappeared. Staying at a hostel in Nassau."

"Any connections to Lyford Cay?" I asked.

"It doesn't say. But it does say that her friend said she had met a man while they were here and that she was supposed to meet up with him when she disappeared. The authorities never found out who the man was."

"A man, huh? Does it say if he was Bahamian or American?" I asked.

Emily shrugged. "Nope."

"Okay, but it still gives us something. What else have you got?" I asked, taking notes on my pad.

"Second victim I found was in 2013, three years later. Also a young white girl, age nineteen, found by a fisherman in the ocean, tongue cut out. Annie Turner was visiting from Mississippi on her high school graduation trip. She was scheduled to fly home on May 30, 2013, but she never showed up at the airport. She was last seen by her classmates outside of Hard Rock Café in Nassau. They said she was hanging out with a couple of local residents. When the three men were questioned, they said they dropped Annie off at her hotel later that same night, and they had no idea what happened to her afterward."

Emily looked up at me and our eyes locked. "One of the men who was questioned was Mr. Sakislov."

I wrinkled my forehead. "Henry's dad?"

She nodded.

"What a strange coincidence," I said.

"Sure is."

43

Nassau, Bahamas, October 2018

"And the third case? You said there were three," I asked. I didn't feel tired at all, even though it was after three o'clock in the morning. This case had just been blown wide open for me.

Emily bit her lip, then nodded.

"Yes. Three years ago, in 2015. Jill Carrigan, age twenty-one, also white, from Arizona was found murdered. She was visiting with a group of college friends on spring break when she disappeared. They were partying downtown, and she met a guy in some bar that she went home with, her friends explained. They never saw her again, and none of them could identify the man, even though they were taken in for a line-up. Jill was found floating in a pool a few days later. Her tongue had been cut out."

"Just like the others," I said. "Whose pool was it?"

"It was at the clubhouse at Lyford Cay."

My eyes grew wide open. "What?"

She nodded.

"Did they have any suspects?" I asked.

"They arrested a man, Juan Garcia, an illegal immigrant who

worked as a gardener in Lyford Cay. He confessed to having murdered all three girls. That's probably why the police haven't been talking about the old cases. But get this, according to the toxicology report, all three of them had hydroxybutyric acid in their blood. Also known as liquid ecstasy. It's a date rape drug. The report concluded it was somehow injected into the girls, probably in their thigh where they all had the same puncture wound. The drug was also found among Juan Garcia's possessions."

I rubbed my forehead. "Oh, wow. So, they did believe they had a serial killer, but that he was arrested?"

"Yes."

"So, someone is in prison for committing these three murders, and we believe he's innocent?" I asked. "A scapegoat."

"Just like Sofia. They could easily have planted that drug to make him look guilty."

"Wow. This is getting bigger than I would have ever imagined," I said, feeling slightly overwhelmed.

But it all made a lot more sense now. The police feared for the American tourism, and therefore they quickly found a scapegoat so that they could close the cases, and people felt safe enough to come visit their little piece of paradise. Then, when a new girl showed up like one did seven months ago, they quickly found someone they else could get to confess. They didn't want to accuse any of the inhabitants at Lyford Cay since their business here was too important and their pile of money too big. So instead, they closed their eyes to the fact that one of the world's most lucrative places to live also housed one of the world's worst serial killers. It had to be someone from the inside. No one else had access to the community. You had to be on the list even to visit.

The question remained, who was he and why was he committing these brutal crimes? I had to start by finding out who the guy was. Several of the girls, it was mentioned, had met some guy. And what did Mr. Sakislov have to do with all this? Had he been a suspect in any of the other cases but the public just didn't know?

I looked at Emily. She gave me one of her most endearing smiles.

"You want me to hack, don't you?"

"I never thought I would hear myself say this, but could you…please?"

She chuckled. "My pleasure. I'll see what I can find in the police files. You go back to your beauty sleep."

44

Nassau, Bahamas, October 2018

"Jack, wake up, wake up."

I blinked my eyes. It was light outside. Emily was looking down at me.

"W-what's going on?"

"I got the files," she said. "I copied them and downloaded them to my laptop."

I sat up. "And you're sure no one can track you?"

She scoffed. "They don't have any security at all to protect their information. I could walk right in…so to speak. I left no trace. I'm sure of it."

I got up from the bed and yawned, feeling exhausted. I couldn't quite grasp how Emily managed to seem so alert and like she wasn't tired at all. Was it an age thing? It made me feel old.

"It's your turn now," she said and handed me the computer.

I grabbed it and sat by the small table. Emily stood close to me, looking over my shoulder as I opened the first file, the case of Laurie Roberts. I read the description of how she was found, then opened the photos taken at the scene. I zoomed in on them, then read the autopsy report and wrote things down on my pad. Emily was still staring at me, and I looked up.

"How about you get yourself some sleep?" I asked. "You didn't sleep at all last night."

She bit her nails. "I don't think I can sleep. This is too exciting."

I chuckled. "That wasn't a request. You need your rest. Detectives need to be on full alert, and you can't be that if you're exhausted. Take a few hours, and then I'll tell you everything I've found out. When you wake up."

"Right," she said. "We work in shifts."

I chuckled again as I watched her crawl on top of her bed and fall asleep as soon as her head hit the pillow. I listened to her light snoring for a few seconds, then shook my head, feeling overwhelmed with love for her. Whatever was going on with her these days, I liked it. A lot.

I returned to the case, wrote some more notes on my pad, then opened the next case. I read through the autopsy, looked at the photos, and wrote down the list of suspects that were taken in for questioning, then continued to the third case and did the same. When I was done, Emily was still deeply asleep. I felt my stomach growling, so I ran down to the restaurant, grabbed us a few plates of scrambled eggs and bagels, along with a pot of coffee and some cups, then hurried back to the room with it all on a tray.

As I walked inside, Emily had woken up. She was rubbing her eyes, her hair standing out in all directions.

"Where were you?"

"Got us some breakfast," I said.

I saw her put a hand to her stomach, then watched the fear creep into her eyes as she spotted the food on the tray.

"This was all they had," I said. "There was no more fruit. I know you like fruit."

She glanced briefly at her suitcase containing the scale and notebook. I didn't know if she had been on it the past few days or if she had kept track in her book, but I hoped she hadn't.

"Do you think you might be able to eat this?" I asked cautiously.

She grabbed her stomach, and I could almost sense how she

scolded herself for having lost control. She looked up like she wanted me to take over, like she was afraid to make the decision herself.

"It won't hurt you," I said, a sadness growing inside of me. It was brutal to see your daughter fight within herself like that. To see how she looked fearfully at something so ordinary as food. Food that was meant to keep us alive.

She contemplated for a few seconds before making her decision.

"I'll just have some coffee…for now," she said.

45

Bahamas, October 2018

Her head was pounding heavily. It started while she was still passed out and sneaked into her dream. But as the pounding grew worse, Coraline finally opened her eyes with a loud gasp. As she did, she looked into a set of familiar eyes.

Feeling confused, Coraline looked around and sat up on the couch.

"W-here...am I...w-wh...what happened?"

The person bent over her and removed a lock of hair from her face. Coraline didn't like it and pulled away. Maybe it was the way this person was staring at her; maybe it was the place or the dream; she didn't know what it was. But something made the hairs on the back of her neck rise.

"I should get...going."

Coraline rose to her feet and stood for a few seconds while trying to maintain her balance. She tried to remember what had happened but couldn't recall anything after she had gotten dressed at the club and looked at herself in the mirror. She wondered if she had gotten drunk, but to her surprise, she didn't even remember a second of the date. Had she gotten anything to eat? She was starving, and her mouth was so very dry. Had they gone to a restaurant? She couldn't recall. Not even a little piece of it.

"How did I get here?" she said and looked around in the windowless room. "What time is it?"

The person sitting on the couch sent her a smile that gave her the chills. Coraline ignored it, then walked forward before she stopped and looked around.

"How do you get out of here?"

"You don't," the person answered.

"Excuse me?" Coraline said.

"You don't."

"B-but…I have to…go."

"No, you don't," sounded the answer, eerily calm.

"But…I…"

The person rose and approached Coraline with fast steps. The look in those deeply angry eyes made her wince and back up.

"W-what do you want from me? W-why am I here?"

"Because I want you to be," the person said.

"I…I want to go home," Coraline said. "Please."

She backed up further till she felt the stony wall behind her. The person came closer and closer, then lifted a hand up, almost threateningly, and Coraline winced again, her eyes locking with theirs.

To her surprise, the hand touched her cheek gently, then caressed it, and her shoulders came down once again. Maybe this person didn't want to harm her after all? Despite the look in those deep-set eyes. Despite the fact that this was a room with no windows or doors. Despite the fact that she felt much like a prisoner.

Coraline exhaled, relieved, just in time for the fist to slam into her cheek so hard she knocked her head against the stony wall before sliding to the ground. The next punches that followed felt like a rain of pain, and soon she didn't feel anything anymore.

46

Nassau, Bahamas, October 2018

Emily was holding her cup between her hands. I felt like a pig sitting there eating my bagel and scrambled eggs, while she had nothing. I kept wanting to ask her again if she was certain she didn't want anything, but I didn't want to ruin the mood. We were doing so well.

"So, what did you find out?" she finally asked, breaking the ice. "While I slept?"

Happy to talk about something else, something that interested both of us, I pulled out my notes. I wiped egg off my lips with a napkin, then started to read out loud.

"First of all, I found tattoos on all three of them. They all looked to be recently made."

"That can't be a coincidence, then," she said and sipped her coffee.

"Exactly," I said, then continued, "All three victims had their tongues cut out as well."

"Which tells us the tongue must have some significance to the killer," she concluded.

I gave her an impressed look. "Yes, but what?"

She shrugged. "He wants to deprive them of the ability to speak, maybe? To silence them?"

"Sounds plausible," I said. "It could also refer to a traumatic event in his early life. In all three cases, it was done while they were still alive. The cause of death in all three cases was suffocation as the lungs were filled with blood."

Emily looked up from her cup. "So, they choked on their own blood?"

I nodded. "I am afraid so."

"Yak."

"I know. It's nasty."

She took another sip. She had that pensive look in her eyes like a million thoughts were running through her mind at once.

"So, he kidnaps them, cuts out their tongues, and lets them bleed to death. Anything else? Sexual abuse?"

I shook my head. "Not according to the autopsy."

"So, the mutilation itself is what gets him off. That's the reason he keeps doing it. He's perfecting it, doing it over and over again. Plus, he has a type; all the girls are similar-looking and have the same origin; they are all American. That must mean he's killing the same person over and over again. Maybe because the real person who is the subject of his anger can't be killed or already has been killed."

"How do you know so much about this stuff?" I asked, quite surprised.

"I've been reading a lot. You have many books around the house about this stuff, and then there is a lot about it online."

"So, you've been reading about profiling serial killers just for the fun of it?" I asked.

She shrugged. "I guess."

"I see," I said, impressed, and looked down at my notes, then back at my daughter. "And what do you make of all this, then?"

She chewed on my question a few seconds, then said:

"The tattoos. I think we need to take a closer look at them. At first, I thought it was because they had all been with the same tattoo artist before they were kidnapped, and that was where he had spotted them, but Nancy Elkington's mom said that Nancy would never go into such a place and her friend confirmed that. I don't think that they had them made willingly. I say the key is in the tattoos."

I leaned back in my chair, feeling one of those proud dad moments. I couldn't believe my daughter was so good at all this stuff.

My stuff.

"Then let's do just that," I said and grabbed the laptop.

47

Bahamas, May 1984

It was time for Dylan's bath, and Carla asked the girl to help her out. She was busy in the kitchen getting a big dinner ready for twenty guests that The White Lady had invited that same night. Even though Carla had all the girls in the house working on it, there were still not enough hands, she complained.

So, the girl drew Dylan's bath, filling the tub in his bathroom upstairs, carefully testing the temperature to make sure it wasn't too hot or too cold. Dylan was sitting on the tiles where the girl had told him to sit, staring at his feet. His toes were dirty from playing outside, something The White Lady hated when he did, but he ran out there anyway. The White Lady had seen him out there and screamed for the girls to make sure he was cleaned up for tonight when all her important guests arrived.

The girl didn't really understand why the son seemed to be more important than the father, who wasn't there and wouldn't be joining The White Lady for dinner with the important guests. Come to think of it, he hadn't been around for months, and several of the girls in the kitchen were whispering about him, saying that he had left, that he finally had enough of all her yelling and bossing him around.

"Do I have to?" Dylan asked. "Do I have to take a bath?"

The girl nodded. "Your mom says so."

Knowing there was no way to get around his mother's orders, Dylan got undressed and stood naked in front of her. The girl looked down at that thing between his legs, then chuckled. It was the first time she had ever seen one of those, and it was quite tiny and wrinkled, she thought. Nothing much to brag about in her opinion.

Seeing her amusement, Dylan covered himself up and blushed, while she helped him get into the warm water and sink his body down.

The girl then grabbed the soap and started to scrub his back and, lifting his arms, she cleaned his armpits and stomach, rubbing them roughly while images of Gabrielle's dead body being carried out of the shed rushed through her inner eyes, like a movie of deep horror.

The girl tried not to, but every time she was near The White Lady, she would think about it. She could feel that anger rise inside of her and found it hard to hold it back. A couple of months earlier, she had ended up losing it and screaming at her at the top of her lungs. The White Lady had stared at her, eyes wide, when Carla had rushed in, grabbed her by the hand, and dragged her out of the living room, apologizing to The White Lady, telling her she would take care of it and punish the girl properly.

Back in the kitchen, she had scolded the girl and told her never to do that again, never to raise her voice at The White Lady again if she wanted to stay alive. The girl had listened to her words, but they hadn't taken root. She couldn't help herself. Every time she was near her, she was filled with such anger, she wasn't sure she would be able to hold it back much longer.

"Ouch," Dylan said and winced.

The girl was pulled out of her train of thought when the boy whimpered and felt his armpit where she had been scrubbing so hard it was turning red and blistering.

48

Nassau, Bahamas, October 2018

"So, I have found all the tattoos and written them down," I said and showed Emily my notepad. "They're all words. Look."

"We know that Nancy's was 'Joy,'" Emily said and came up behind me to look over my shoulder.

"If we take them in the order they were killed, then we have Laurie Roberts. On her back was a tattoo with the word PLEASE. She was followed by Annie Turner who had the word PANIC on her back. And finally, we have Jill Cardigan who had the word CHURCH tattooed to her chest."

"And Ella Maria?" Emily asked.

I shook my head. "I haven't been able to find any pictures of hers, and it's not described anywhere in any reports. Maybe it was in a place where it was well hidden. We would need to see the body to find it, and that might be a little hard by now."

"Okay, so we leave her out of it. For now. So far, we have the words Please, Panic, Church and finally, Joy," Emily said. "Those are all very odd words."

"I know, and it would be easy just to conclude that they're random, but I think they must mean something," I said.

"How come this wasn't a part of the investigation?" she asked. "How could they have missed this?"

I shrugged and put my feet up on the chair next to me. "Maybe the police here didn't think it was significant. They might not even have mentioned it to the parents."

"Or maybe they did, and the parents felt embarrassed that their daughters had a tattoo like that, maybe they thought that she had been hiding it from them and then just never said anything," she added.

"I wonder if there's a connection between these words," I said pensively.

"We can try and put them together in different orders to see if they create something, if the killer is sending us a message," Emily said.

I did as she told me to and put the words in random order, then switched them around, but nothing seemed to make any sense. I rubbed my forehead and finished my coffee that had gone cold when my cell suddenly started to ring. I picked it up.

It was Commissioner Maycock.

"Great news!"

"How so?" I asked, surprised to hear him so cheerful.

"We have caught the killer."

"Excuse me?"

"Nancy Elkington's killer. We have him in custody. He was bragging to all his friends, telling them about the body in the swampy waters. That's how we found him."

"Found who?" I asked, sensing this was going somewhere terrible.

"The boy. You were right. He did exist. His name is Jamie Davis. He's a local boy."

"You arrested the boy who found the body and then ran away?" I asked, almost unable to breathe.

"Yes indeed. He confessed to everything."

"Even to cutting her tongue out?" I asked.

The commissioner went quiet for a second. "Well, yes, of course. Anyway, we are on our way to tell her parents. I should think they would be very happy. Case is closed. You're free to leave if you need to."

"I...are you sure about this?" I asked, wondering how on earth this man could be so terribly blind.

"Yes, yes. I have a signed confession."

"And what about all the other killings? The boy can't be any more than fifteen, seventeen at the most."

"What other killings?" the commissioner asked, then added a tsk. "Just be happy, will you? Case is closed. We can all sleep well now. Weather is good. Sun is shining. Go chill on the beach."

I hung up, thinking that if he thought I was able to sleep well or even chill anywhere after he yet again had arrested an innocent for what this serial killer was doing, then he was fooling himself.

I looked at Emily with a deep sigh.

"Now what?" she asked.

"I think I need to visit Juan Garcia in prison. After three years in jail, he might be willing finally to speak."

49

Bahamas, October 2018

Coraline could hardly open her eyes. They were swollen and painful. She woke up lying on the tiles, still in the windowless room. Coraline sat up. She tasted blood in her mouth. She wiped her nose and realized she had a nosebleed. Coraline started to sob.

How did she end up in this mess?

You trusted the wrong guy. Meghan told you this would happen, didn't she? She warned you, but you wouldn't listen.

Coraline thought about her friend. Would she know that she was missing by now? Coraline had the day off, so it wasn't like she would be missed at the club. She lived alone, so no one would miss her at home either. Would her mother maybe call? It wasn't very likely since she hadn't called Coraline much since she met her new husband, Greg.

Greg was a software developer with his own company and hundreds of people working for him. He was a self-made man, who had worked so much in his younger years that now he had just sold his company and received almost a hundred million dollars for what he had spent the past ten years building. So now, he wanted to see the world, he had told Coraline's mother when they met through a dating app.

"And I want a companion."

It hadn't taken Coraline's mother many seconds to say yes, and now, that was all they did. Travel all over the world to exotic places, forgetting all about her daughter and everything else back home.

It wasn't that Coraline didn't think her mother deserved this newfound happiness; she totally did. Her dad hadn't exactly treated her well in the divorce, and she had been miserable for many years. She had then turned to drinking and, soon after, Coraline had seen a side to her mother that she didn't care for much. That side was gone now, so that was the good news. The bad news was that Coraline missed her mother and now that she had gotten herself into some deep trouble, she needed her more than ever.

"There has to be a way out," Coraline mumbled to herself as she got back on her feet. She tried to look through her beat up eyes, to search for an exit somewhere, but all she could see were walls and more walls. At the end of the room was a bathroom but that had no windows either.

"If there's a way in, there's a way out," she reassured herself, walking into the bathroom and looking around. In the ceiling, she spotted a ventilation duct. Could she possibly open that and crawl up there?

Coraline stared at it, then down at her body. She was short, but not exactly light. Over the past year, she had gained a lot of weight on her butt and thighs. Her arms weren't strong enough to pull her up. She'd have to find something she could stack, or maybe there was a chair that could help her reach?

Coraline looked around inside the room again, then found one by the corner. It wasn't a very tall chair, more like a fancy recliner, one of those designer ones you only saw in magazines.

Coraline grabbed it with her bruised hands, then pulled it, straining her back. She placed it directly underneath the duct and then stood on the chair. She reached her arms up toward the ceiling. Coraline breathed in excitement.

If she stood on her tippy toes, she could touch the duct.

50

Nassau, Bahamas, October 2018

Juan Garcia's brown eyes rested on me across the table. We were sitting in one of the barren rooms at the prison the next day. It was early in the afternoon, but in there, it might as well have been in the middle of the night. I wondered when Juan had last seen daylight or even felt the sun on his skin.

I had just told him I didn't believe he killed those three women.

Juan Garcia's brown eyes stared at me from a dirty face. I wondered from the smell of him if showers were even offered.

"It doesn't matter."

"I think it does," I said. "I've looked into all the three cases, and they bear too many similarities to two recent cases, which were committed after you were incarcerated. I think the killer is still out there and you were just used as a scapegoat, giving them someone to blame."

Juan smiled an almost toothless smile, then shook his head. "You're looking for justice? There is no such thing."

"Yes, there is," I said. "If you help me."

"How? How can I possibly help you? Look where I am."

I leaned forward. "You signed a confession; why?"

Juan shook his head and leaned back. "It was a very long time ago."

"I have a feeling you still know why you did it," I said, "why you signed the papers."

Juan looked down like he was ashamed and that was when it struck me.

"You can't read, can you? You didn't know what you were signing?"

Juan lifted his eyes, and they met mine. He didn't have to answer. The look in those eyes was more than enough. I felt my heart rate rise as the anger settled inside of me. This man had been wrongfully imprisoned for three years just because he couldn't read what he was signing.

"I was illegal," he added. "Came from Ecuador. I traveled through Colombia, where I paid all I owned to be put on a boat and promised to reach America. But I ended up here. It is many years ago now. They gave me a job, food to eat, and a roof over my head. But I never learned to read."

"You were a gardener, right?" I asked.

Juan's face lit up. "Yes."

"At Lyford Cay, right?"

He nodded eagerly like the memories of the great outdoors made him forget where he was for just a few seconds.

"Who did you work for?"

Juan smiled. "The White Lady."

"The White Lady?"

He nodded with a shiver. "That's what we called her. She told us we didn't need to know her name. To us, she was either ma'am or simply Mrs. When she wasn't listening, we just called her The White Lady because she always wore those white dresses and scarves on her head. Scary woman."

"I take it she didn't treat you well?" I asked.

Juan scoffed for an answer when a thought struck me.

"Did she tell you to sign those papers?" I asked, leaning forward again. "Was she the one who told you to do it?"

Juan spat on the floor, then looked up at me, fire in his usually so-gentle brown eyes. Once again, he didn't have actually to say the words for me to understand.

51

Nassau, Bahamas, October 2018

When I returned to the hotel, it was crawling with police. Six police cars were parked outside, and my heart immediately dropped. My first thought was that something had happened to Emily.

I parked and rushed into the lobby, where Commissioner Maycock was standing, flirting with the receptionist. When he saw me, he straightened up and forgot about her.

"Detective," he said and approached me.

"What's going on?" I asked, still frightened half to death. "Has something happened?"

Maycock became serious, then nodded. "I am afraid so."

Oh, dear God!

"There has been another one," he said.

"Another one?" I asked, still thinking it was about Emily.

"Another girl gone missing," Maycock said, pulling me aside so the receptionist wouldn't listen in on our conversation. "American."

Relieved that it had nothing to do with Emily, I exhaled, but then the seriousness of the situation sunk in, and I looked at the man in front of me. For the first time, I sensed he too was feeling helpless.

"We need your assistance, Detective," he said. "We want this to stop."

I nodded pensively. "I will help you, but I have a couple of conditions."

Maycock nodded. "Anything."

"First of all, you let the boy go. Jamie Davis had nothing to do with the murder of Nancy Elkington. He's nothing but a young boy who was in the wrong place at the wrong time. He's still just a suspect, so it should be easy to simply let him go home."

Maycock thought about it for a few seconds.

"I'll deal with the Elkingtons," I added, knowing that was probably his biggest concern. He liked being able to tell the relatives that he had solved the case. It was less fun to have to tell them he was wrong.

"Okay," Maycock said.

"Good. Also, I need access to all your files, autopsy reports, toxicology reports, medical examiner's reports, and so on. Everything you have. No questions asked."

"Naturally."

"Good. Now, the thing is, I have very good reason to believe there is a connection between the killings of Nancy Elkington and Ella Maria Chauncey and the three girls that the gardener Juan Garcia is in prison for murdering. I can't prove anything yet, but I want to work on this theory. You have a serial killer on the loose, and I believe that killer is connected to Lyford Cay."

I waited for Maycock's reaction before continuing. I knew the neighborhood was a no-go in his world; it was untouchable, but I was determined to change that.

"What I need is full access," I said. "To the neighborhood. I need to be able to come and go as I please. No more lists. No more alerting people before I arrive. I drive up to the gate, and they let me in without questions."

Maycock looked like I had told him I wanted to marry his daughter and take her to the moon.

"Now...that is..."

"Those are my terms," I said. "They are not negotiable. I am the one with experience in catching serial killers, and this is the way I can do it. This guy is accelerating right now; he's on a killing spree, and we need to stop him."

"But…Lyford Cay?"

I nodded. "Yes, Lyford Cay. Full access. Whenever I want."

The commissioner swallowed and looked at me with wide eyes, sweat springing from his upper lip.

"All right. But we keep this between you and me. No one else can know we're looking at a serial killer. It's bad for tourism."

I chuckled, then placed a hand on the man's broad shoulder.

"You've got that part right. Now, if you'll excuse me, I need to go get my daughter. We have a killer to catch."

PART IV

52

NASSAU, BAHAMAS, OCTOBER 2018

They sent over a guy with all the information on the girl who had gone missing, and I read through the missing person's report with Emily.

"Her name is Coraline Stuart, age nineteen," I said. "Picture fits the profile. Blonde and American. Worked as a waitress at Lyford Cay Clubhouse, where she was last seen two nights ago as she was getting dressed for a date. Her co-worker, Meghan, saw her in the dressing room and spoke to her."

"Again, we're back to that place," Emily said. "Everything seems to circle around that neighborhood."

"Sure does," I said.

"Who reported the girl missing?"

"Her mother sprang a surprise visit on her two nights ago, flying in with her millionaire husband. They hadn't seen each other for a year, and the mother thought it was about time. She tried to call her once she landed at Nassau Airport, then grabbed a taxi to her apartment, where she found she wasn't home. The mother then called the friend, Meghan, and she told her that Coraline was going on a date with a guy. So, the mother found the spare key that her daughter always kept under the mat outside because she always forgot her keys, so she let herself in. When the daughter didn't come home all night, she grew worried. She tried calling her again and again all day long, and someone did pick up suddenly. But it wasn't her daughter on the other end; it was another worker at the club-house who had found her phone in the trash can. He also found Coraline's purse in there, and that was when the mother became worried. She went to the police and filed a report."

I looked up. "And since they've just had another girl go missing and turn up dead, they took it very seriously, which is good. Usually, they would have told her to wait and see if the girl showed up on her own."

"So, the Royal Bahamian Police Force did some good police work for once," Emily said.

"I should say so," I said, "and it will be to our advantage. The earlier we react, the faster we can find her, hopefully still alive."

"I can't stop thinking about the guy she was dating," Emily said. "It's been a theme in several of the cases, hasn't it? That she was meeting up with someone on the night she disappeared?"

I nodded. "Yes. Except Nancy. We don't know if she met up with someone maybe secretly or met her killer randomly. And Ella was with Henry."

"True. Oh, wait, I forgot...there was another thing," Emily said. "I noticed it when you were gone, and I read through the reports. Annie Turner was last seen with Mr. Sakislov and his friends, right?"

"Uh-huh."

"Well, I read through Jill Carrigan's report."

"The one who met someone at a bar and went home with him? But her friends were too drunk to be able to ID him?"

"Yes, there was one witness at the bar who said she saw them leave in a Rolls Royce. She said she remembered it well because that is a very rare car around here."

I nodded, thinking I had always dreamt of driving one of those.

"Okay, and?"

"Well, I looked it up, and guess who owns a Rolls Royce like that…?"

I looked at her, not very surprised.

"Sakislov?"

"Bingo."

53

Bahamas, May 1984

"You're hurting me."

Dylan squirmed and pulled away from the girl. She stared at his armpit where she had been scrubbing and at the blood oozing from the small blisters and scratches. His big eyes stared at her, and as she looked into them, they reminded her of his mother. Again, she saw that face who had beaten her with the grater until she fainted, who had beaten Carla, and who had killed Gabrielle. Again, she heard that scraping sound of Gabrielle's nails against the metal door. And again, she noticed the metallic taste of anger in her mouth. Everything about him disgusted her.

"You filthy animal!" he yelled.

The girl stared at the boy, so pale, so fragile, with most of his body sunk into the water. She felt such hatred at that moment, such deep anger, she grabbed him and pressed his head down. Her hand pressed harder, and the boy slid under the surface of the water. His body squirmed, his arms and legs flailing as he fought underneath the surface. She held him down, pressed his head under the water and made it stay there, being older and much bigger than he was. Dylan's eyes looked back up at her as she held him down.

And then she smiled at him.

After a while, his arms and legs stopped moving, and now they were just floating aimlessly in the water. The girl felt a great calm spread throughout her body, a peacefulness unlike any she had ever experienced. Like all the screaming voices, all the scraping sounds were silenced all at once.

She felt happy.

The girl tilted her head and stared at the lifeless body underneath the rippling surface and placed her head on the edge of the cold bathtub, staring down at Dylan, who now lay completely still. The girl put her fingers in the water and ran them across the surface. She liked watching Dylan in the water. She liked looking at those lifeless eyes staring back up at her.

The girl sat in silence until she heard footsteps coming from outside the door. Realizing what she had done, she reached down into the water, almost panicking, and pulled Dylan up. The door soon opened, and Carla stormed inside. She took one look at the lifeless Dylan in the girl's arms, then rushed to them and pulled him forcefully away from the girl.

"H-he fell," the girl said, but she could see in Carla's eyes that she didn’t believe her.

Carla placed Dylan on his back on the tiles and blew air into his lungs. She then pressed on his chest, whimpering and calling his name.

"Please, Dylan, Please."

Even though nothing happened, Carla didn't give up. Frantically, she continued to try and blow life into the boy.

"Come on, Dylan, wake up," she said and slapped his face, hard. Then she turned her strained face and looked at the girl. "Do you know what you’ve done? She's gonna kill us; do you realize that? The White Lady is going to kill us!"

The girl swallowed but, to her surprise, she felt no remorse; she felt no regret. She stared at the lifeless boy in Carla's hands in fascination and awe.

Finally, on Carla's third try, Dylan coughed, and water spurted out of his mouth. Carla breathed a sigh of relief. While Dylan came to himself, she scolded the girl.

"Don't you ever do anything like that again, you hear me?"

Then she turned to look at the boy.

"It was an accident; you hear me? It was nothing but an accident! Don't you dare tell your mother otherwise."

Dylan nodded while coughing again.

"W-what happened?" he asked, looking confused.

Carla sighed in relief once again. "You don't remember. That's good. That's very good. Now, let's never talk about this again, okay?"

As Carla spoke, the girl stared at the boy. Their eyes locked for just a few seconds and, by the look in his, and the smile that went with it, she knew that he remembered what she had done.

He remembered very well indeed.

54

BAHAMAS, OCTOBER 2018

Coraline panted and strained to crawl up into the duct. She could barely fit and thanked God she hadn't inherited her mother's wide hips. At least not yet, even though the past month's weight gain did point in the wrong direction. When growing up, she had always dreaded that she would one day get her mother's figure and her mother had told her she might, once she had children. Since then, Coraline had been exercising regularly to keep those hips at bay and tried her best to keep fit so she never would. She had even promised herself that after she had the three children she dreamt of having one day, she would make sure to exercise so she didn't end up like her mother.

Gosh, how I miss her.

Coraline was overwhelmed by sadness when thinking about her mother and how badly she wanted to see her again, how she wanted her to take her into her arms and just hold her there, to protect her from all this evil.

How did I get myself into this mess? How did it come to this? How could I have been this stupid?

She also thought about how silly she had been for being so

angry with her because she wanted to live her life, because she wanted to travel and remarry. Coraline's dad had treated her terribly in the divorce, not wanting to give her any money and almost rubbing it in her face how wealthy he was when she wasn't. Why wouldn't she grab the opportunity when it presented itself? Why shouldn't she? Coraline just wanted her to be happy, she realized, and if that was what it took, then so be it. She had just been selfish and wanted her mother to be available for her when she needed her, not thinking that her mother might have needs of her own to think about.

I am sorry, Mama.

Coraline managed to squeeze herself into the small hole and crawl forward. It was dark inside the duct and Coraline had never been good with tight spaces. She whimpered as she pulled herself forward into the darkness, dust and dirt getting inside her nostrils and touching her fingers.

She slid her body through the darkness, feeling so dirty she wanted to scream, not knowing where she would end up. Coraline continued till she saw light, then rushed to reach another end, kicked the covering open, and slid out. She fell to the tiles and hurt her shoulder in the fall. A scream of pain slipped out, even though she was trying her hardest to hold it back.

She lay still for a few seconds, listening. She pondered if she could hear any footsteps or voices approaching. There seemed to be nothing but the sound of a grandfather clock leaning against the wall, tick-tocking away, telling her that time was passing, and she needed to hurry.

Coraline looked around. The stone walls were covered with wooden shelves holding bottles of wine from top to bottom. In the middle stood an old slap-wood dining table and at the end of that table was something that made Coraline sick to her stomach.

An old skeleton was sitting in the chair. Coraline approached it, shivering in fear. On the table in front of the skeleton was a jar with something in it. Coraline walked closer to see better, and when she saw the cut-out tongue inside the liquid, she turned around and threw up bile on the brown Spanish tiles.

55

Lyford Cay, Bahamas, October 2018

"You told the police she was going out with someone, a man. Do you know who he is?"

Meghan Williams sniffled. Her eyes were red from crying. Emily and I had found her at the clubhouse at Lyford Cay. The commissioner had kept his word to me, and I had been able to get right in without being on any list or even stating my business in the neighborhood.

Meghan shook her head. "I…I just know she had been seeing him for a while. She never told me who he was."

"But you also stated that you warned her against him," Emily said and walked closer. She had been keeping her distance, staying out of my talk with the girl, just like we had agreed. But now she was breaking our agreement, and I sent her a look. Emily ignored it.

"You must have believed he was dangerous or at least not good for her?" she continued.

She was making a good point; no, make that a great one actually, and the question was spot-on, but I still would have preferred that she hadn't meddled. I was the only one who was a detective here, and she was, after all, just a young girl with no authority. Luckily, Meghan didn't question her presence.

"I knew he wasn't good for her," she said. "That's all."

"How did you know if you don't know who he is?" Emily asked, coming closer to Meghan, who was sitting on a bench in the dressing room, where another co-worker had found Coraline's phone and purse. Emily sat next to her while waiting for her response.

"I…I…saw him…" Meghan said. "Once. He was picking her up in his car. I don't want any trouble," she then said, looking around nervously.

"I think you'll be in bigger trouble if you don't tell us," Emily said. "This guy might be a killer, and if he knows that you know who he is, he'll come after you next."

I stared at my daughter. She was right, but I thought it was a little harsh. Still, it worked. Meghan looked at her with a frightened look on her face.

"Listen," I took over. "All we need is a name. Then you're off the hook."

She shook her head again and looked down. "I…can't."

"Because he's a regular here?" I asked.

She nodded, her head still bent.

"How about we just say a name," Emily said, "and then you nod if it's him? Would that work?"

Meghan sniffled, then looked up.

"He'll never know it was you, and technically, you won't actually have said anything," she said.

Meghan nodded. "Okay."

Emily gave me a look like she wanted me to take over. I approached Meghan and knelt in front of her. Her hands were shaking as she wiped her nose with the tissue.

I exhaled. "We think it might have been Sergei Sakislov…are we right?"

Meghan sniffled and looked at Emily, then back at me.

Then, she nodded.

56

Bahamas, October 2018

The person was standing in the doorway. The door in the wall was opening slowly, as usual, sliding to the side, revealing the existence of the room that you wouldn't know was there.

In his hands, he was holding the equipment. The bag with the ink, the needles, and the butcher's knife, barely cold after the last victim.

The person chuckled as he entered the room and looked around, his eyes searching for the girl.

"Where are you, little girl?" he said as the door closed behind him at the touch of his hand on the stone.

"Are you hiding, huh? Well, two can play that game."

The person put the bag down with a chuckle. This girl wasn't the first to try and hide from him. A lot of them had done the same. He couldn't blame them. At first, they thought they could escape, but as they realized there were no doors or windows, that's when they panicked and usually tried to hide. But the person knew all the hiding spots in the room, so it wasn't a game that would go on for very long.

"Ready or not, here I come," he said, chuckling.

The person walked to the couch and looked behind it, remembering that was where he had found the first girl he had taken down there. She had been all curled up against the wall, covering her head with her arms, whimpering. It was her whimpering that had led him to her immediately.

The person grabbed the couch and pulled it away from the wall with a loud roar.

"GOTCHA!"

But the girl wasn't there. Of course, she wasn't. The person shivered in delight. He liked this little game. It made it all a little more exciting. He liked it when the girls didn't give up, when they fought for their lives a little. It made it more fun. The ones that gave in quickly were boring, and he would usually finish with them pretty quickly. It just didn't give him the same kick. Luckily, most of the girls he had gotten over the years were feisty.

Just like this one.

He knew her name, but he didn't want to say it out loud. He didn't like to think of them as humans, as people with names. These girls were his toys; they were his little pets, his fun in a dull and tedious world. He owned them and could do to them as he pleased.

"You better hang tight to your hiding spot, little girl, ‘cause I’m coming for you!" he exclaimed and walked toward the bathroom, where he thought he saw a foot sticking out behind the toilet bowl. Originally, there had been a door there, but since he had a girl down there who had hidden in the bathroom and blocked the door, he had removed it so it wouldn't happen again. It had been a lot of trouble getting her out of there.

"I’m coming, ready or not!"

The person approached the bathroom, then peeked inside. As he stared at what he had believed was the girl, he realized it was something else entirely. It was the chair from the living room, which she had dragged inside the bathroom, and the thing he thought was a foot sticking out was actually the front of the ventilation duct from above.

As the person stared at the open duct, he clenched his fists on both hands so hard he dug his nails into the skin. He rushed to his bag, then took the knife in his hands, and stormed for the door.

"So, that's how you wanna play, little girl, huh? Then let's play."

Barely had he made it out of the room and closed the door behind him before he heard the doorbell ring.

57

Lyford Cay, Bahamas, October 2018

"What can I do for you, Detective…Ryder, was it?"

His maid had shown us into Sergei Sakislov's study. He was sitting by his giant desk, while thousands of books were towering on shelves behind him. From the ceiling above us hung a massive chandelier that I could only assume was made from real diamonds. I would be disappointed if it wasn't since everything else in this huge mansion seemed to be *over the top*, as my mother would put it.

I sat down in a leather chair. Emily grabbed the one next to me. Sergei Sakislov's eyes rested on my daughter for a little too long in my opinion.

"We're here regarding a missing girl."

I placed my phone on his desk and pushed it toward him with Coraline's picture on the display. I watched him look at her, then pretend like he didn't know her, but the small twitch around his right eye told me he did.

"Haven't seen her," he said and pushed the phone back, then gave Emily another look.

"We have reason to believe you know her," I said.

He smirked, his eyes not leaving Emily. I felt like punching him.

"Really? Well, I know a lot of...girls around here."

"I bet you do, Mr. Sakislov, but there's a little more to it than that," I said. "We have reason to believe that you were supposed to meet with her on the night she disappeared."

His eyes were now on me and the smirk was gone. "What on earth do you mean?"

"You picked her up from the clubhouse, didn't you?" I asked. "You were dating her, and then you decided to kill her, am I right?"

Mr. Sakislov stared at me while running a hand through his long gray—almost white—hair. He was dressed like someone who thought he was at least twenty years younger. The half-buttoned shirt showed a very hairy chest underneath, which he was obviously very proud of but would probably have made most women run away screaming if he hadn't had the wealth to make up for it. His skin was covered in some sort of glitter on top of the suntan.

"Why do you come here...in my own home...accusing me, Detective?" he asked.

I leaned forward. "Because I think you killed her, just like I think you killed Nancy Elkington and Ella Maria Chauncey and three other young girls before them."

Mr. Sakislov stared at me again, then laughed.

"This is joke, no?"

"It is no joke, Mr. Sakislov," Emily took over. She pulled out a file from her bag and put it on the table, then opened it.

"What I have here is the transcript of Ella Maria's phone calls in the days before she died. And, lo and behold, if you don't appear on that list of numbers several times just in the three days up until she died."

Mr. Sakislov leaned forward in his chair. "I have a son who dated her. It must have been him."

"He's lying."

The voice came from behind us. I turned and watched as Henry Sakislov entered the study, rushing toward us.

"Henry?" his dad said. "What are you doing here?"

"I'm here to tell the truth, Dad. And you should too."

58

Lyford Cay, Bahamas, October 2018

"You must excuse my son; he doesn't know…he's so heartbroken over losing his girlfriend, he doesn't know what he's saying," Mr. Sakislov tried.

"Yes, I am heartbroken," Henry said and approached us. As he did, I could tell he had been crying.

"But not only because she's gone."

"Don't listen to him," Mr. Sakislov tried again. "He's not been well."

"I am very well, Daddy Dearest; don't you worry about that. It's him you shouldn't listen to," Henry continued. "He's the one who's lying."

"Enough!" Mr. Sakislov said, slamming his hand onto the desk. "Enough of all this nonsense."

Henry shook his head. "No, Dad. This is not one you can just yell or pay your way out of. Don't you think I know? Don't you think I know what you did to her?"

Henry was trying to hold back the tears, but they kept streaming across his face. He was pointing his finger at his dad.

"You slept with her. With my…*my* girlfriend. The one thing I had in my life that was mine. You took it from me; you took her from me."

Mr. Sakislov exhaled and rolled his eyes. "I don't have to listen to all this..." He rose to his feet, but his son rushed to him and pushed him back into his chair, then stood above him, a clenched fist in front of his face.

"You took her; you destroyed her. I wanted to marry her; you just wanted to...to play with her. The way you play with every girl you meet. It was the one girl you shouldn't have touched, the one that was mine, yet you couldn't keep your hands to yourself, could you? It doesn't matter who they are...if they're black or white. You just see a girl and have to have her, don't you? Just like you have to own everything else. Like all this...this...worthless crap," he said and threw out his hands. Admit it, Dad. You slept with her. Don't you think I know that was why they hated us? Why she wasn't allowed to come here anymore? I found out when I read some of the texts she wrote to you, and I saw a picture she had sent of herself...naked. Yet I still stayed with her because I loved her. Something you have never been capable of. But I could never be you, and you were all she wanted."

Mr. Sakislov exhaled. "Okay. If that's what you want to hear, then yes. I slept with her. A few times. But she came to me, son. She wanted to be with me. I didn't go after her. She told me she wanted to do something crazy; she wanted to be wild. I guess what you could offer her wasn't exactly enough."

As the last word fell, Henry took a swing at his dad and punched him on the cheek, hard. I think it surprised him just as much as it did his dad because he let out a small whimper, looked at his hurting hand, then turned around and ran out of the room.

Mr. Sakislov felt his cheek, then gave Emily and me an angry look, his enormous nostrils flaring.

"Get out."

He rose to his feet, still holding a hand to his throbbing cheek, then yelled at us.

"Get out of my house. If I ever see your face in here again, it better be with a warrant!"

59

Bahamas, October 2018

Coraline heard steps. At least she thought she did. She was standing in the wine cellar, staring at the skeleton, shaking, when she heard it again. This time closer. The steps seemed angry and determined.

Someone's coming.

Coraline gasped and looked around to find the exit. There was only one door at the end of the room, only one way in and one way out.

There is nowhere to go.

Quickly, Coraline threw another glance around the room and then—as she heard noises coming from the other side of the door—she rushed to one of the shelves and pulled out a dusty bottle of wine to use as a weapon.

She waited by the door as it opened, then as a face peeked inside, she swung it so hard, the person never knew what was coming. There was a thud as the bottle hit the person's forehead, but the bottle remained intact. The man fell to the floor, face first, and Coraline hurried out into the hallway, not even looking down at him.

She ran as fast as she could down the stony hallway until she reached a set of stairs and could see a closed door at the end of it. She took the steps two at a time as she rushed up toward the door, hoping and praying that it wasn't locked.

Please, dear God. Please, let it be open.

As she reached halfway up the stairs, she felt something grab her ankle, and a second later she was forcefully yanked down, slamming her face against each and every step.

Coraline screamed as she was pulled downward, then looked up toward the door, blood filling her eyes from a wound in her forehead, when she saw the door above slide open, and a figure stood hovering on top of the stairs, a figure looking much like an angel in white clothing in the light coming from behind.

"Help!" Coraline exclaimed, reaching out her hands toward this angel, while forcefully being pulled down.

But the angel wasn't there to help, she soon realized. Instead, she closed the door behind her and walked down the steps, balancing on her high heels, while the man behind Coraline pulled her down onto the floor in the hallway. As the pulling stopped and Coraline felt the cold tiles against her cheek, she heard voices above her, distant foggy voices speaking in an agitated manner.

"How did she get out? How could you let this happen?"

"She climbed through the ventilation duct."

"Well, get her back in there and finish it up. We need to get rid of her. The ground is burning under our feet."

"Yes, Mama," the man answered.

"Well, why are you just standing there? Get her out of here!"

"Yes, Mama," the man repeated and, soon after, Coraline felt a pull on her feet as she was dragged across the tiles. She wanted to scream, she wanted to yell at them for treating her like this, she wanted to fight, but her head was pounding so terribly, and she felt so extremely dizzy, she could hardly even…think. Coraline sent signals to her brain to tell her legs to kick, to kick the guy hard and run again, but her legs didn't obey. Instead, she watched through a curtain of blood as her traitorous body was dragged back toward the room, and through an opening in the stone wall. She was placed on the floor and, as the door in the wall closed behind her, she realized she wasn't alone. The man had stayed inside with her.

60

Bahamas, May 1984

"Did you really think you'd get away with it? Did you really think I wouldn't find out? That my son wouldn't tell me?"

The White Lady was fuming as she stood in the kitchen, staring at Carla. The girl was sitting by the counter, cutting carrots when they entered. It was just her and the boy. Dylan stood in front of her, looking at the girl with a mischievous look.

Carla wiped her hands on her apron, then turned around to face The White Lady.

"Answer me, woman!" she yelled at Carla.

Carla didn't look up at her. She stood with her shoulders slumped, staring at her worn out shoes.

"I…I don't…"

"You tried to kill him, didn't you? You wanted him to drown in that bathtub."

Carla raised her fear-struck eyes, then shook her head violently.

"N-no."

"Don't lie to me now. He told me everything. You tried to drown him; then, when it didn't succeed, you told him never to tell on you."

Carla shook her head again. "N-n-o, ma'am, that's not..."

"Oh, I am done with your lies. I'm sick of them, to be honest," The White Lady hissed. "I have done so much for you. You were my favorite. I let you go into town. I risked my life by letting you do that. If you were found by an immigration officer, they would have come for me too; you do realize that, right? I've risked my own life for you. For you. I trusted you. And this is how you repay me? By trying to kill my son?"

"N-no, I didn't...I..."

Carla glanced quickly at the girl. The girl winced and shook her head. She clenched the knife between her fingers.

"Look at me when I am talking to you!" The White Lady yelled.

Carla did. She sighed.

"I'm sorry," she said.

The White Lady threw out her arms. "Oh, she's sorry now, is she? The woman tries to murder my son, and now she says she's sorry?"

Carla stared at her feet. "Yes, Ma'am. I am very sorry."

The girl stared at her, small gasps leaving her lips.

"Oh, I'll give you something to be sorry about," The White Lady said.

She then reached over and grabbed the knife out of the girl's hands. She grabbed Carla by the hair and forced her to her knees, holding her face toward the ceiling.

"Dylan, come here," she hissed, and the boy obeyed. He rushed to his mother and stood beside the kneeling Carla.

"You want to keep silent about things?" The White Lady said, strained. "Well, say your final word and then keep silent forever."

"No, Please...I..."

Dylan's hands were shaking as his mother handed him the knife. She then reached inside Carla's mouth, grabbed her tongue and pulled it out between her lips, forcefully. Carla whimpered and sobbed while the girl watched, holding her breath.

As the knife swung through the air and cut Carla's tongue off, the boy lifted his head and locked eyes with the girl. In that second, they shared a moment that would forever determine the course of their lives.

As the knife cut through the flesh and the thick veins, Carla sank to the floor, blood gushing out of her mouth.

"Leave her there," The White Lady said and walked to the door with a grunt.

After she had left, the two children sat on the cold floor, holding hands across Carla's bleeding body, watching her sputter and gargle as her lungs were slowly filled with her own blood.

61

Nassau, Bahamas, October 2018

"How on earth did you find out about the phone numbers?" I asked and looked at Emily. We had left Lyford Cay and were driving toward downtown. "Did you hack again?"

Emily chuckled. "Nah. It was a lucky guess."

My eyes grew wide as we approached Nassau. "You bluffed? There were no transcripts?"

She shook her head. "Nope."

I had to laugh. "You've got some nerve, young lady. I am impressed."

"Can you believe the guy, though?" she asked and shivered. She looked at me. "So, you think he has Coraline?"

"I feel pretty confident that he does. If he hasn't killed her and gotten rid of her body yet, that is."

I drove up in front of the police station and stopped the car.

"Well, if he does have her, then we have no time to waste," she said and placed a hand on my shoulder.

We walked inside and didn't even stop when the secretary told us the commissioner was busy. We just walked straight in. Inside, we found Maycock at his desk, a woman sitting in his lap, kissing him.

I pushed Emily behind me.

"Dad, I'm nineteen," I heard her mumble while I cleared my throat. "Excuse me, Commissioner, we have an urgent matter to discuss."

The commissioner let go of the woman, then smiled widely at us. "Detective Ryder. It is good to see you."

He's not even embarrassed?

The commissioner was still smiling as we approached him. He winked at the woman, and she got down from his lap, wiped her lips, and rushed past us.

As she left and closed the door behind her, the commissioner clasped his hands.

"She needed to pick up the kids anyway. They're at my parents' house."

I gave him a strange look. "She's…that was…your wife?"

The commissioner nodded and smiled widely. "Yes. Mrs. Maycock," he said proudly. "Now, what can I do for you, Detective?"

I exhaled and leaned forward. "We need a warrant and as many officers as you have on hand."

The commissioner lifted his eyebrows. "You have evidence?"

"We know where Coraline Stuart is being kept," I said.

"Let me guess, somewhere in Lyford Cay," the commissioner said with a deep sigh.

I nodded. "Yes, and we need to move fast. I don't know if she's still alive but every moment that passes is one minute more he can use to kill her."

"And just who are we talking about?" he asked.

I swallowed, bracing myself for his reaction.

"Mr. Sakislov."

The commissioner's eyes grew wide. "Oh, no. Oh, no. No. No. No."

"Before you refuse, you must hear us out. I know he's an important guy around here. I know he owns the biggest piece of land in Lyford Cay. I know he puts a lot of money into your country. I know you've renamed an entire point for him, but I am telling you, it all adds up. He had a date with Coraline on the night she disappeared. He was the last person to see her alive. We have a witness who said she was supposed to meet up with him. He was also questioned in connection with the killing of Annie Turner in 2013 and, according to his son, he was sleeping with Ella Maria Chauncey behind the son's back."

"And Nancy Elkington?" the commissioner asked. "Did he see her too?"

I shook my head. "We don't know. We don't know if he was connected to Laurie Roberts either, but the files said she met someone. The same goes for Jill Carrigan, who went home with a guy who drove a Rolls Royce. We don't know if it is Sakislov, but he does own a Rolls Royce."

The commissioner rose to his feet and closed his jacket over his big stomach with a grunt. He pointed a finger at me.

"You better be right about this."

62

Bahamas, October 2018

Coraline felt hands on her body and was turned around. She felt powerless in the hands of this man, this predator who stood above her, looking down at her with those fiery eyes.

"Please," she said with a whimper. "Please."

The pleading didn't seem to help her. Actually, it had the opposite effect.

"I don't want to die, please," she continued nonetheless.

The man leaned forward and wiped blood from her face, then said with a low voice, "But you will. Don't worry. In just a few minutes, it'll be all over."

"No," she said, crying. "No. Why are you doing this?"

The man didn't answer. He grabbed his bag and started to pull out some things. Coraline watched him through blurry eyes as he pulled out needles and ink.

"What are you doing with those?" she asked, remembering seeing similar equipment in the tattoo parlor she had gotten that small heart she had on her ankle when she turned eighteen, much to her dad's regret.

The man now walked to her, then started to unbutton her shirt and pull it off. Coraline tried to fight him, but he held her down, and soon she had to give up. Next, he grabbed her pants and pulled them off. As he spotted the tattoo on her ankle, he stopped and looked at it.

"Huh," he said. "I prefer an empty canvas…" he paused and looked up at her with a smile. "I guess this will have to do."

He turned her around so that he could look at her back, then ran a hand slowly down her spine.

"Some might say it would be easier just to write the word on your back," he said, "using a permanent marker. I understand why they would say that, but since you'll be left in water, I prefer making it more permanent, if you know what I mean. Why water, you might ask? Well, I prefer it because it removes all traces like fingerprints and any DNA I might leave behind."

"P-please," she continued.

His hands were still examining her body, touching the skin all over her back and then turning her around and feeling the skin on her stomach. Coraline was crying heavily now, and soon those cries turned to screams.

The man shook his head. "You really think anyone can hear you? This room is the safest place on the planet. The walls are so thick you couldn't even drill through them."

Coraline still screamed with all the strength left in her small body.

The man searched her stomach, then paused.

"Yes, I think this is the spot," he said. "Right here on your stomach. Now, it might hurt a little bit, but I am sure you won't feel it since you'll be…well, almost dead when I start doing it. Usually, it takes around two to two and a half hours for someone your size to bleed to death, choking on your own blood. So, don't worry; you will hardly feel the needle as I decorate your body. Besides, you'll probably pass out pretty quickly from all the blood loss."

The man looked at her, then reached over and grabbed a butcher's knife. Coraline saw it, then whimpered and tried to crawl away, but the man grabbed her by the feet and pulled her back toward him. He then turned her around and looked down at her, holding the knife close to her face.

"Now, say your final word," he said. "And make it a good one."

63

LYFORD CAY, BAHAMAS, OCTOBER 2018

It was with great satisfaction that I handed over the warrant to Mr. Sakislov. Meanwhile, what seemed like the entire Royal Bahamian Police Force entered the resort-sized house and started their search.

"They're not gonna find anything here," Mr. Sakislov said, still fuming. "You're wasting your time."

"Let me be the judge of that," I said.

"What's going on?"

Henry Sakislov came out in the great hall that was the size of the three-bedroom apartment where I used to live.

"What's going on?" he asked again. "Dad?"

"They think I murdered Ella," he said.

Henry's eyes grew weary. "Murdered her? No," he said addressed to me. "You misunderstood. He's a playboy; he sleeps with young girls and treats them like dirt, but he's no killer. He didn't kill Ella."

"Just let us do our job," I said. "We have reason to believe he might have killed several young girls around the island."

"Tell them to hurry up. I'm hosting a party tonight," Mr.

Sakislov said. "And I don't want your men crawling all over the grounds."

I stared at the son, wondering what kind of grown-up he was going to be with an upbringing like this, with a dad like this.

"Where is your mom?" I asked. "Is there a Mrs. Sakislov?"

"There was. There have been several," Henry answered and sent his dad another look. "But none of them stuck."

"So, where is your mother now?" I asked. "Could you go and live with her in case we need to arrest your father?"

"You're not arresting anyone here," Mr. Sakislov snorted.

"But just in case we do find something, and we have to take him in," I continued. "Could you go live with her?"

Henry looked down at the marble tiles beneath him, then shook his head. "We hardly know one another."

"And it won't be necessary," his dad said.

"Again, let me be the judge of that," I said just as the commissioner came back in the hall followed by a flock of his men. He looked tired and sweaty, and his eyes told me he didn't carry good news. As he approached me, he started to shake his head.

"Nothing. We found nothing."

I didn't see it because he was standing behind me, but I just knew that Mr. Sakislov was smiling from ear to ear. I could almost hear his smirk from where I was standing.

"Keep going," I said.

"We've been everywhere," the commissioner said. "There is nothing, no sign of the girl."

"Try again," I snorted, sounding almost like Mr. Sakislov. "Keep trying!"

"As you wish," the commissioner said, and they disappeared once again. I could hear them running around from room to room and from guesthouse to guesthouse outside, searching up and down while I was standing inside the great hall, suddenly sweating quite heavily.

64

Lyford Cay, Bahamas, October 2018

"Nothing."

Commissioner Maycock threw out his arms as he repeated the word for the third time. We had been there for several hours now, still with no luck. I stared at him, sweat prickling on my skin. I could feel Sergei Sakislov's piercing eyes on my back.

"You hear me? There is nothing here," the commissioner continued. "No Coraline Stuart, none of her clothes or belongings. Nothing that could have belonged to any of the many girls you believe had been kept here before they were killed. Nothing."

The word echoed inside my head, and I felt like screaming. This couldn't be correct; it simply couldn't. I had been so certain.

And yet I wasn't. A small part of me knew it was too easy of an answer. But I had wanted to believe it. I sure did.

Mr. Sakislov approached us, then leaned over with the biggest smirk I have ever seen and said: "Now, if you'll please leave my property before my guests arrive."

I couldn't stand his self-righteous face. I didn't know what was worse, the triumphant look in his eyes or the gloat in his voice. Maybe they were equally terrible.

"Go on, go," he said and almost shooed us out like we were dogs or sheep.

I did feel kind of sheepish; I had to admit.

Outside in the street, as the gate closed behind us, Commissioner Maycock approached me, his eyes scowling.

"I am sorry," I said. "I was so certain."

"You're off the case," he said. "Done."

He sounded like I was one of his employees that he had just demoted. I felt compelled to remind him that I was actually here on my vacation and had helped him out on this case of my own free will and because he needed me, but I didn't. Instead, I nodded in agreement.

"We'll deal with this ourselves," the commissioner continued. "You've embarrassed the entire Royal Bahamian Police Force. You've harassed a perfectly innocent man."

"I wouldn't call him *perfectly* innocent..." I said.

Maycock lifted his finger to make me stop.

"You have brought us nothing but trouble. Mr. Sakislov is a very important contributor to our country."

"Again, I am sor..."

Commissioner Maycock shook his head.

"Maybe it would be best if you and your daughter left tomorrow. Go back to your hotel now. I will send for a car to make sure you make it to the airport tomorrow. Good night."

With those words, the commissioner turned around with a grunt, then walked to his car where one of his officers was holding the door for him. The car shook as he got in, and a second later, they drove off.

I glanced at Emily. How had I messed this trip up so terribly? I had completely lost track of why we were here originally, and now we were being forced to leave.

"I ruined everything. I am sorry," I said to her as we walked toward our rental car, the warm evening air embracing us like blankets.

Emily looked up at me, then wrapped her arm under mine.

"I'm not," she said.

65

NASSAU, BAHAMAS, OCTOBER 2018

For once, it wasn't only Emily who had no appetite for dinner. As we sat in the hotel restaurant, neither of us touched our food or spoke. It was game night at the hotel, and they were showing a college football game featuring local Bahamian teams.

Halfway through my conch fries and beer, my phone vibrated in my pocket, and I picked it up. The number on the display was American.

"Ryder here."

"Jack, it's Irene."

"Irene, hi," I said.

"I have taken a look at the email you sent me."

Irene was a well-known FBI-profiler who I knew from my days back in Miami. I had worked with her on many occasions when trying to profile a killer. She was the best in her field. I had completely forgotten that I had written to her about the case a few days earlier.

I sat up straight. "Yes, and?"

"I've spent all day thinking about it and then, just a few minutes ago, it struck me. The words tattooed on the girls' bodies. They are your clues. I think they are their final words."

"Final words?" I asked when something happened in the game, and everyone stood to their feet, cheering. I signaled to Emily that I was going to walk away to hear better, and she nodded to let me know she understood.

"How did you come to that conclusion?" I added as I found a spot by the hotel pool where I could hear better.

"It's the first word that gets to me," Irene said.

"Please?"

"Yes. It sounds like something you'd say right before you die, right? It fits with the fact that he cuts out their tongues. You know to silence them forever. Anyway, it's just a theory. Something for you to work with."

"But..." I said. "They don't seem to make sense. The words. What is he trying to say?"

"As I said, it is just a theory, but..."

"Yes?"

"Maybe it's not the killer but the victims that are trying to tell you something," she said. "Listen, it was just a thought. I gotta go now, but let me know how this ends, okay?"

I hung up and stared at the phone for a few seconds. Could she be right? Were the victims really trying to tell me something? In that case, what? What did the words mean?

I walked back to Emily.

"The game ended, and everyone is going home," she said. "I think they won. They all seemed so happy." She studied me as I sat down across the table from her. "What's wrong?"

I explained to her what the profiler had told me, and she got that pensive look on her face once again.

"I can understand 'please,'" I said. "And 'panic' even, but what about the others?"

"Church and Joy?" she asked.

"Yes. What are they supposed to mean? Is it religious?"

She stared at me, biting her lip. "I don't think panic is something you'd say right before you die. You might yell help, no, or please, but not panic."

"Good point," I said and sipped my beer. "Maybe Irene was wrong."

Emily's eyes were flickering back and forth. I could tell she was thinking about something. She grabbed her phone and began to type. Then she grumbled something and typed something else.

"What?" I asked. "What are you thinking?"

Emily smiled and looked up from her phone, then turned it so I could look at the display.

"I'm thinking that Irene is right. She is so right."

66

Nassau, Bahamas, October 2018

"How could I have been this stupid? How could I have been this ignorant? The answer was right in front of me the entire time!"

I was rushing through downtown Nassau, running every red light I came across.

"That goes for the both of us," Emily said.

I gave her a look. My smart daughter.

"Okay, then we. How did we not see this? I mean, how did we not think about the fact that Church was a high-end English shoe brand of hand-made luxury leather shoes and that Joy by Jean Patou was a perfume worn only by the extremely rich since it costs around six hundred dollars per bottle?"

"Known as the costliest perfume in the world," Emily added. "And the very perfume I saw in the bathroom at the Chauncey's house when I was there hanging out with Sydney."

"That combined with the fact that Mrs. Chauncey, aka The White Lady, was so busy finding a scapegoat to take the fall. It always struck me as odd," I said. "I mean, why would she tell Juan to sign a confession? Why would she force Sofia to?"

"Because she was hiding something," Emily said. "Maybe even covering for someone, probably her husband."

"I have a feeling we're onto something," I said and drove up to the gate with the big sign saying Lyford Cay.

I rolled down the window so that the guard could see me. "Hi there, Jason," I said, recognizing him from earlier.

"We need to get back in, please."

Jason got up from his chair and approached the window. "No can do, I'm afraid."

"Excuse me?"

He shook his head. "I am sorry, Jack. I have strict orders not to let you in again."

"But…Commissioner Maycock…"

He shook his head again. "I can't let you in. You've been banned from ever entering Lyford Cay again. Maycock told us this."

"You're kidding me. I'm a detective. There's a girl…she's in there, and…he'll kill her if you don't let me in."

"I am sorry," Jason said. "My hands are tied."

I stared at the man behind the thick glass. I couldn't believe this. Why did this have to happen now? Now that we were so close?

I sighed and backed out of the entrance area, then left.

"Where are we going?" Emily asked. "Dad, you gotta help the girl. You've got to get in there."

"I will," I said and accelerated down the street.

"How? Maycock won't help you. He wants you gone; you know that. He'll send a car tomorrow to make sure we're going to the airport."

"It'll all be over by then," I said.

I followed the large wall enclosing the neighborhood closely, then turned the car down a small trail toward the beach and stopped as we reached the sand.

Emily looked out the window, then back at me.

"What are we doing here? There's no one here. How will you save Coraline? Sydney's in that house too; we need to help her, Dad. How will you do that?"

"I have my ways," I said and got out of the car, then stared at the big ocean in front of me, where the moonlight was glistening on the surface.

The ocean.

My friend and companion through all my life. The big dark blue.

Once again, you're going to be my savior.

67

Nassau, Bahamas, October 2018

The small diving shop was closed, but someone was still in there closing up. I saw the lights, then pulled the doors and knocked when I realized it was locked. The shop was located on the beach in a small wooden shack. I had noticed it before when driving by.

"Hey," I said, knocking hard on the glass. "Could you please open? I need your help."

The man looked in my direction. "We are closed, sorry."

"No, please, this is urgent."

The man hesitated for a few seconds, then walked to the doors. I placed my badge in the window, so he could see I wasn't someone there to rob him.

"Police, American."

He turned the lock and opened the door. "American, huh?"

I nodded. "Yes. A girl is in danger, and I need some equipment."

"I can't. It's after closing time; I am sorry," the man said. "Come again tomorrow."

I pulled out my wallet. "I have money."

That seemed to do the trick. The guy nodded eagerly as I

handed him a couple of hundred-dollar bills and he told me to take whatever I needed.

"What are you doing, Dad?" Emily said as I approached the tanks and picked up a set of fins.

"A boat they'll notice even if it is dark out. There are cameras at the docks. If I come in under water, they'll never see me."

"You can't be serious," she said, crossing her arms in front of her chest.

"Oh, I am very serious," I said. "I'm going in."

She shook her head. "No, not about that. I meant you can't seriously think I'll let you go in alone?"

I looked up at her. "Oh, no. You're not going with me, you hear me? You stay here and wait for me."

She grabbed a set of fins and looked at them. "These should fit me. Now, I just need a snorkel and tanks."

"I am serious, Em. It'll be dangerous. Don't be naïve."

"I am nineteen years old, Dad; how many times do I have to tell you? You're the one who is naïve if you think you can do this without my help. You're the one who always tells me that two are better than one. I'm not letting you go in there alone, and that's the end of this discussion."

Seeing the look on her face made me chuckle. She almost looked like my mother. I wasn't happy about bringing her since I feared something bad might happen to her, but at the same time, I couldn't blame her for wanting to go, and I kind of liked that she did want to go. This case was as much hers as it was mine by now. Maybe even more hers than mine. Besides, Emily was a good scuba diver, and I should know since I was there when she took her certificate.

"You really shouldn't go in the water at this hour," the owner said. "It's dark and shark feeding time."

I helped Emily find a mask that fit, then put my own gear on before I looked at him.

"We'll take the chance."

68

Nassau, Bahamas, October 2018

I had always heard that diving at night opened a door to a new world of adventures, even when visiting sites you had dived a dozen times before. This was mostly due to the fact that there was a shift in the environment's inhabitants as nocturnal creatures emerged while the familiar fish and ocean life disappeared. It was also due to the fact that the diver's perspective changed at night. During the daytime, divers tend to look at the big picture, seeing whole swaths of reefs and frequently miss many of the smaller things. But at night, the limited visibility narrows your focus.

I had never been in these waters before, and I had never dived at night either. I didn't tell that to either the man in the shop or Emily. After going over the signals and ways to communicate with one another, I sunk myself into the black waters, Emily following close behind. And that was quite different than what I had previously experienced during my diving trips to the Keys. Very different. The feeling of the darkness surrounding me, enveloping me completely, and the fact that I couldn't see more than a hand's length ahead of me made it creepier than anticipated.

I tried my hardest not to show Emily just how anxious I was and continued forward, making sure she was close behind. As we walked out far enough into the water, we began to swim, going as fast as we could, using the flippers to propel us forward. I could hear my own racing heartbeat as we shot through the water.

Every now and then, I surfaced to see where we were and make sure we stayed close to the shore, which made it less frightening somehow. Not that there wouldn't be bigger fish there, because there were. We saw them swim past us, but often when it was too late to get out of their way. A huge grouper swam right toward me at one point and looked like it wasn't going to divert when I shined my light on it, and then it decided to go above me instead at the last minute.

I gasped inside my mask, then turned to look at Emily, who had remained calm. She signaled thumbs up, and I responded with one as well.

Then we continued.

I was breathing heavily and, as I pushed forward, a school of mutton snappers fled from me. Further ahead, I spotted more snappers and even a lionfish. And, of course, we saw dolphins, a big pod of them. I think I scared them and wondered if they had been asleep when I came by. They took off so fast, stirring up the waters, you'd think there had been hundreds of them when there were probably just ten or so. It was hard to tell in the darkness.

I surfaced and could now spot Sakislov's huge Inca-inspired resort-style estate just around the point. I knew we had only about half an hour left, maybe less, and dove underwater again to signal Emily. When I shone my light toward her, I noticed she had frozen in place. She was pointing at something behind me. I twirled in the water as fast as I could, and now I saw what she was seeing.

A great white swimming eerily close to us.

I let out a shriek, then swam to Emily and signaled for her to stay calm. We watched the shark for a few minutes as it slowly approached us, my heart beating rapidly in my chest.

I knew that the most important thing was to maintain our composure; it was the key to staying safe. The majority of shark attacks on humans were simply a result of them mistaking you for another animal.

I knew all of this to be true, but as I watched the big animal approach us and knew it could easily gobble us up, I found it harder than anything in this world to remain calm.

I wanted to turn around and swim away, screaming.

I knew that, many times, the sharks would just swim away, uninterested in the diver, that's what I had read, but this one seemed not to have gotten the memo. The shark came up close, a little too close for comfort.

I could tell Emily was about to lose it. She was squirming and whimpering behind her gear. I stayed in front of her, in case the shark decided to attack; it could take me down instead of her. I just prayed that she wouldn't panic. I knew that erratic movements could get the shark's attention and provoke it. Frozen stiff, I forced myself to breathe slowly.

Please, just go away. Please, go away.

The shark came so close I was certain I could have reached out and touched it. I didn't do it, naturally; I didn't move an inch or even blink as it came so close, like it was curious, like a dog wanting to smell us, then suddenly decided against it and took off.

As fast as it had appeared, the shark was gone. Emily and I both breathed, relived, and, still shaking, we swam the rest of the way, constantly fearing it would be back for us, feeling like it was right behind us, just waiting for the moment to attack.

Luckily, that was all just in our imagination and, minutes later, we were able to crawl up on the seawall belonging to the Chaunceys' million-dollar house.

69

Bahamas, October 2018

He was holding the girl down. She was squirming underneath him, making it hard for him to keep her still. She was bleeding from the bruise on her forehead, and blood was being smeared all over his gloved hands.

"Fight all you want to, little girl," he groaned while trying to keep her head down, pressing it against the tiles. "It's no use. I will have my way sooner or later anyway."

Finally, he managed to press her head down and break her feistiness. As she groaned and moaned beneath him, trying to get loose, he leaned all his weight on top of her, pressing down till she became completely still. He had done this so many times before; he knew exactly how it would go. As time passed, she would eventually give up. It was all about breaking them. When the time came, and he was certain she had no more fight in her, he leaned forward and whispered.

"Now, say your final word for me."

He waited, but no word left her lips, only deep growling.

"Come on, girl. Tell me your final word," he said, angrily pulling her head backward so that he could look into her eyes.

"What will it be?"

The girl stared at him, her eyes wide, her face strained from being pulled backward. But still, she refused to say anything. Her nostrils were flaring, her teeth gritted, but her lips never parted, and no sound came across them.

"Tell me!"

He pulled her hair to bend her head even further backward, and the girl let out a deep groan as he pulled it hard, but there were no words.

"TELL ME!"

He was yelling angrily now, but still, the girl didn't comply. She simply refused to tell him her final word. He let go of her hair, and her head fell back down. The girl was sobbing now but didn't use any words.

Well, this has never happened before.

He had never thought about the fact that one of them might refuse to speak. They usually always did at some point. They usually ended up yelling it out in despair, probably thinking this meant he would stop torturing them, not realizing that he had only just begun.

He had to admit, he didn't know what to do.

He looked at his watch. It was getting late. He had to finish this before morning; otherwise, he'd have to wait another day, and Mama was determined to get them out of there as quickly as possible. He couldn't blame her. The police had gotten a little too close, not the Bahamian police with that idiot Maycock in charge, of course not. But that darn detective from Florida who had come looking for relatives for his daughter. What kind of bad luck was that anyway? To have him come snooping around here? Mama had yelled at him for letting them stay alone in the house while he went golfing, but how could he have known? He didn't exactly present himself as a detective. Besides, Mama was in the house while they were still there and could keep an eye on them and make sure they came nowhere near the basement.

It wasn't his fault the guy turned out to be a detective, was it?

Mama seemed to believe so, but then again, she believed everything was his fault.

The person stared at the needles next to the girl and the ink, then decided he didn't have to wait for the girl to say her last word. He could simply take the last one she actually had said to him earlier. Just use that one and end it all. He had lost interest in this girl anyway.

What was it she had said to him last?

Oh, yes. *Please*. Please was the word. It wasn't very original, but it would have to do.

The person lifted the butcher's knife and locked eyes with the girl. He grabbed her face, then reached inside her mouth with his gloved fingers. He searched around, then finally managed to grab ahold of her slippery tongue, pressing down hard so it wouldn't slip out of his fingers. Then he pulled it out between her lips, forcefully, and the girl almost threw up.

He then lifted the knife into the air and locked eyes with the girl, feeling that intoxicating adrenalin rush through his body, arousing him. As the knife swung down toward her tongue, he almost screamed out his arousal. In that same second, the alarms went off on his phone, letting him know someone had just entered his house. The person stopped the knife in mid-air as the blaring alarm destroyed everything. His arousal, the adrenaline, the kick.

The person looked at his phone where the security cameras showed him a man and a young woman walking through the sliding doors in the formal dining room. Recognizing them immediately, he sighed, then let go of the girl, who curled up on the floor, sobbing. He rose up, then turned and walked outside, the knife still clutched in his hand.

70

Lyford Cay, Bahamas, October 2018

"I don't think anyone is home."

Emily turned around and looked at me. We came in through the unlocked sliding doors in the formal dining room, and now we were in the massive kitchen. What was the plan? To find Coraline and liberate her. If she was still alive. And hopefully get Sydney out of here along with her. Then we'd have to deal with Mr. Chauncey afterward. Hopefully, the police would help us if we brought the girl back and she could tell where she was and who had kept her.

If she was still alive.

"Let's try upstairs," I whispered.

We found the stairs in the grand hall and walked up, then continued down a hallway decorated with stunning artwork.

We found the master bedroom and entered as soon as we realized no one was in there. Emily closed the door behind us, then looked at me.

"What are we doing here?"

I searched a few drawers, opened cabinets, and peeked inside the Roman Empire-style bathroom, then returned to her.

"Looking for clues."

"This place is massive," Emily said. "Coraline could be anywhere. Shouldn't we be looking elsewhere? Why are we in the master bedroom? What are we looking for?"

I stared at a door, then opened it, revealing an enormous walk-in closet the size of my living room. I entered, walking down the rows and rows of neatly ironed suits on one side and the completely identical white dresses on the other. At the end of it was a mahogany wall filled from top to bottom with hundreds of drawers. In the center was a safe behind a wooden door.

"Why are you so interested in a safe?" Emily asked, looking worriedly behind her. "I don't understand...wait, what was that?"

"What was what?"

"I thought I heard a sound," she said with a light gasp. "Please, Dad, hurry up whatever it is you're doing."

"It doesn't matter. I can't open it anyway."

I sighed and closed the door.

"I can."

The sound of the voice coming from behind us made us both turn our heads. In the doorway of the walk-in closet stood Sydney. Emily smiled and sighed, relieved.

Then they hugged.

"What are you guys doing here anyway?" Sydney asked as she approached the safe and knelt in front of it. She glanced at our outfits. "Are you wearing wetsuits?"

"Can you really open it?" I asked, ignoring her first question.

She shrugged. "I know all of Mr. Chauncey's passcodes. I grew up here and have been watching him all my life. I know my way around this house better than anyone," she said, then typed in a code, and the safe immediately clicked open. "Here you go. What are you looking for?"

I looked inside the safe, then reached in and pulled something out. I held it up for the girls.

"Bingo."

Both girls looked frightened as they stared at the object in my hand.

"A gun?" Emily asked.

"I knew a man like Mr. Chauncey would have one. We'll need it," I said and got up. As I turned around, that was when I saw something else. It was hanging on a mannequin's head. I walked closer and touched the long silver wig. Emily came up behind me.

"So that's how he made it appear that Sakislov was always near the girls he abducted. A wig, huh?"

"It makes sense," I said. "Everyone knows he's a womanizer, right? In the file, he stated that he never met Annie Turner when he was questioned. We assumed the police were just stupid for believing him, but what if it was the truth? What if he never did meet her? Or any of the other girls?"

Emily glared at me quickly, then back at the wig. "It makes total sense. They hate each other. Mr. Chauncey wanted his neighbor to take the fall. But every time, he managed to avoid being a suspect, probably by paying off the police, and then Mr. Chauncey's wife had to bail her husband out by bringing in the scapegoat as soon as the police started to sniff around or pay any attention to them."

"So, she must have known what he was doing," I said. "She must have known all along."

We both looked at Sydney, who was standing right behind us, staring at us like the moon had fallen down.

"W-what are you guys talking about?"

I grabbed her by the shoulders. "We need to get you out of this place. But first, we need to find Coraline. Is there any place you don't go? Anywhere they say is restricted for you to go?"

"I can't leave the house or the property," she said and looked down. "Because I am an illegal. I was born here, but my mom is here illegally. She came here from Colombia many years ago. But if I leave the house, I'll be arrested, they say."

I stared at the girl in front of me, flabbergasted. "They're keeping you a prisoner here?"

She shrugged. "It's the same for all the workers. We live in the rooms in the back house. They lock them at night, so we don't do something stupid. The farthest I have been from this place is the clubhouse when my mom took me there when I was younger. But I am not really allowed down there. My dad was another worker here. He died when trying to run away. The White Lady shot him."

I stared at the girl while clenching my fingers around the gun. These people were seriously beginning to tick me off. It wasn't the first time I had heard about rich people getting illegal immigrants to work for them, keeping them as slaves. Not so long ago, a woman in Texas had been caught doing the same thing. The poor women she had kept at her house were malnourished and badly beaten when they were found. I knew millions of illegal immigrants ended up as slaves one way or another, whether they ended up in the sex industry or like here as slaves for those who didn't want to work themselves, those who believed they were allowed to keep people and treat them however they liked just because they had money.

"Is Mr. Chauncey the one who tells you that you can't leave?" I asked.

She shook her head. "The White Lady is."

"Of course," I said. "She runs the show around here."

I let go of the girl's shoulders, then looked at Emily, who once again had that look on her face like she was coming up with something, figuring something out.

"Panic," she said, pointing at me.

"What do you mean, panic?"

"It was one of the words tattooed into the girl's body."

"Annie Turner, yes," I said. "What about it? You figured out what it means?"

"She's trying to tell us where she is," Emily said. "Don't you see? It's like it was with the two others. Church and Joy. Two names of something giving the killer away but could also be something else. They couldn't say it directly because the killer would know what they were up to, trying to give clues, so they tried to hide it, tried to give a vague clue. One he wouldn't figure out. This is the same."

I shook my head, suddenly feeling very old because I couldn't follow her.

"I don't see it. I really don't."

Emily clasped her hands. "I know where Coraline is," she said, then turned to face Sydney. "You know this house better than anyone. Is there a panic room or a shelter anywhere?"

Sydney nodded.

"In the basement, why?"

71

Bahamas, October 2018

Coraline couldn't believe her luck. Finally, God was hearing her many prayers and had granted her a break. The man was gone. Something had disturbed him just as Coraline had given up, just as she had felt the fingers clench around her tongue and seen the blade of the butcher's knife swing in front of her eyes. While he was pulling her tongue forcefully and holding it there so he could better cut it, something had happened. An alarm had sounded on his phone and this—whatever it was—had made him let go of Coraline. She had sunk to the tiles, her tongue throbbing painfully from the violent treatment, but it was still intact.

She could still taste his plastic gloves, though, and it made her want to throw up.

Now, as she was lying on the floor, gathering her strength to get up, she wondered if she once again might be able to go through the ventilation duct, but then decided against it. There was no other way than the one that led to the wine cellar, and it took too long. The guy would be back and find her as easily as he did the first time. There had to be another way, a faster way for her to get out.

God, if you gave me this chance, then grant me the wisdom to know how to get out too. I don't think you gave me this miracle, this second chance, if you didn't also provide a way out for me.

Coraline got up and staggered to the stone wall. She had seen him come through it several times now and knew it opened, but how? Coraline placed both palms on the wall and tried to push it with all her strength, but nothing happened.

Of course, it wasn't that easy.

In deep pain, Coraline pushed one stone after another, knowing that the button was there somewhere, even though it was well hidden. She was sobbing because of the pain in her body and the fear of not making it out in time, and she pressed and pulled at each and every stone she could reach, but nothing happened.

"Please, God," she said and slammed her fist into the wall, crying, then sunk to the floor. She was sitting on her knees with her head bent down when the wall suddenly began moving in front of her like her tears had moved it somehow, or she had said a magical word.

Open Sesame.

Eyes growing wide, heart beating fast in her chest, she expected to see the man's face on the other side, but much to her surprise, it wasn't his glaring eyes that appeared as the door slid open.

72

Lyford Cay, Bahamas, October 2018

When we reached the basement, Sydney stopped in front of a large stone wall. Sydney looked at it, then felt the stones one after another. I had explained to her that we were looking for a young girl who had been kidnapped and we believed Mr. Chauncey was keeping her here and that we were hoping to find her alive.

It didn't take Sydney long to find the button to open the secret door. As it slid open, she looked back at us confidently.

"I've seen him go in here before."

As the door was fully opened, we rushed inside. I ran across the floor to the bathroom and looked inside, holding up the gun in case someone tried to attack me. When there was no one in there either, I ran back into the room, shaking my head in desperation.

"No one is here?"

"Coraline?" Emily yelled, but as expected, no one answered.

"Coraline?" I repeated.

"Coraline?" Emily tried again.

I threw out my arms. "She's not here."

"She was though," Emily said and looked down at the floor beneath me. "Look at your feet."

I did and realized I had stepped in a small pool of blood. There was a trail of it leading toward the door.

"They took her out. They must know we're here," I said and held the gun tighter in my hand. I rushed out of the room again and down the hallway, where I kicked open a wooden door and entered what appeared to be a wine cellar.

In the middle was a dining room table and someone—or rather something—was sitting at the end of it.

I approached it, holding the gun up and looking around me to make sure there weren't any surprises to suddenly jump out at me.

"Yuck," Emily said coming up behind me, staring at the old skeleton and the jar with the floating tongue in it.

"What the heck is this?" I asked, looking at Sydney. "Or let me rephrase that, *who* is it?"

73

Lyford Cay, Bahamas, March 2003

At thirty years old, the girl had grown both beautiful and strong. Working in the house or helping out in the yard while growing up had given her strength like none of the other girls possessed. She was also tall, taller than any of them, and she was smart. Listening in on Dylan's private lessons had taught her everything she needed to know to outsmart everyone else.

Being only a few years younger than her, Dylan followed her around, admiring every step she took and listening to everything she had to say. Soon, she learned she could easily twist him around her little finger, and life at the house was beginning to get quite comfortable for her. She no longer dreamt of leaving or running away to find her biological family. Her family was here now, in this house where she had spent most of her life. And as long as she had Dylan, who adored everything about her, she was quite happy.

Almost, that was. Every now and then, she could still taste the metallic anger in her mouth, and it was becoming a nuisance. It happened mostly around The White Lady. That was when she would see the pictures in her mind of Carla lying on the floor, bleeding to death, and hear the scraping sound of Gabrielle's fingernails against the metal door, so loud it almost hurt her head.

The girl stood outside the wine cellar and waited for Dylan as he showed up, grinning that goofy grin of his that he always did when seeing her. He approached her, then grabbed her by the waist and kissed her, sticking his tongue down her throat. The girl kissed him back. She enjoyed his touches and their occasional sex in the basement or the pool house.

"You ready for this?" she asked him as his tongue left her mouth.

He nodded. "It's time."

She was sitting at the end of the old wooden dining table as they both entered. Dylan closed the heavy door behind him and, as it was shut, The White Lady looked up from her newspaper, a disgusted look on her face.

"Ah, it's you two. What do you want?"

Next to her on the table stood a glass of wine that she sipped before returning to her newspaper, obviously not interested in getting an answer to that question.

This was part of her routine. She always had a glass of wine in the cellar while reading her newspaper before bedtime.

"Make it quick," she said, still not looking up.

"Mama?" Dylan asked.

She lifted her gaze, then sipped her wine before forcing a smile. "Yes, darling."

He grabbed the girl's hand in his. "I...we have something we would like to tell you."

She stared, repulsed, at their hands, then gave them a look of disapproval.

"We're in love," Dylan said.

The White Lady stared at them. First, her eyes landed on Dylan, then the girl, then back at her son. A tic started to form in the corner of her eye when she suddenly burst into laughter.

As the laughter subsided, she wiped her eyes and said. "No, you're not. Now, go."

Dylan stepped forward. "But, Mama, please, listen to us."

"No. I will not," she said, then stared at the girl, pointing her finger at her. "Vermin. You're nothing but vermin, disgusting pests that should be eradicated. I should have gotten rid of you a long time ago."

"But, Mama, please," Dylan said, stepping forward.

The White Lady rose to her feet. She walked to the wall, where an old army saber was hanging. It was her grandfather's, she had once told the girl, and she wanted it on the wall to remind her of him, *the old bastard.*

Now, she was taking it down from the wall, slowly, then looking at her son. "Dylan, son. One day, you'll learn that there's a difference between these people and you."

"What are you saying, Mama?" he asked as The White Lady approached the girl with the saber between her hands, her eyes fixated on the girl.

"Mama? What are you going to do?"

"I'm going to end this once and for all," she said, walking closer. "No son of mine will be seen with…with vermin like her."

As she approached the girl, the girl didn't move. She wasn't afraid of The White Lady, at least not enough to want to show her. She stood her ground and stared down at the smaller woman dressed all in white, while thinking of all the hours she had spent in her room locked behind bolted doors, crying and fearing The White Lady's wrath. She thought about all the times The White Lady had beaten her, and of all the other girls and women she had hurt or even killed. And that was when she realized this had to end now. The house—enormous as it was—wasn't big enough for the both of them.

As The White Lady swung the saber at the girl, the girl reacted quickly. She reached out her hand and grabbed the woman's arm. While looking into her eyes, she bent her arm backward and, when pushed, The White Lady dropped the saber. She grunted, annoyed, then threw herself at the girl, but the girl was both bigger and stronger, and soon she had her pinned to the ground, holding her down with both arms.

"Quick," she said. "Grab the saber."

She then reached inside The White Lady's mouth and pulled

out her tongue, pulling so hard the old woman screamed. Then, as Dylan returned with the saber, she looked up at him, and their eyes met in a rush of arousal and excitement.

"Cut it off," she said, sweat springing from her forehead. "Cut it off. Do it NOW!"

Dylan's nostrils flared, and his cheeks turned red as he swung the saber through the air and it cut through the tongue. The sound of it slicing through the flesh and the veins would haunt the girl for years to come, but only as a delightful shiver when remembering her first kill.

Just like they had done with Carla, the two of them watched The White Lady bleed to death on the cold floor, while holding hands over her lifeless body, and this time they both knew this was a defining moment in their short lives. One they would always try and return to, to revive that feeling of total power.

They decided to place her at the end of the table and put her tongue in a jar, to always remind them of how it all began.

But before they did, the girl stripped the old lady of her white dress, becoming who she had always dreamed of being. As she put it on her own body, Dylan stared at her in awe, smiling from ear to ear.

"You answer to me from now on, you hear me?" the girl said, and Dylan nodded.

"Yes…Mama."

74

Lyford Cay, Bahamas, October 2018

"All I know is that she was The White Lady, the first one."

Sydney looked up at me, then back at the dead woman. "My mom told me they killed her."

I stared at the girl, not quite fitting all the pieces to this puzzle completely yet. "So, this is Mrs. Chauncey?"

Sydney nodded.

"And now there's a new one?"

She nodded again. "Mr. Chauncey was the first White Lady's son. I never met her, but my momma told me she was terrified of her. She wasn't as bad as the new White Lady, though. Not according to my momma."

I stared at the skeleton, then at Sydney, while trying to figure it all out. The woman in front of me had been dead for quite some time. I shook my head. Maybe the details didn't matter right now. The guy killed his mother, yes, but worst of all was that he had Coraline and there was no telling what he was capable of doing to her. And besides, whoever this mysterious new White Lady was, she was dangerous. There was no doubt about it. She needed to be stopped.

"We should call the police," I said and found my phone when I heard a sound coming from upstairs. It was followed by a scream.

Emily and I locked eyes.

"Coraline."

Gun clutched in my hand, we rushed up the stairs and into the kitchen, then stopped to listen. I wanted to know where the sound was coming from, but now everything was completely still.

"Where are we going, Dad?" Emily asked.

"Sh," I said. "We need to listen."

"But it's all quiet," she said. "And the house so big she could be anywhere. How will you…?"

I shushed her again. I was certain I had heard something, but then it all went quiet again.

Until I heard an engine roar.

"The garage," I said, panting, and looked to Sydney for guidance. "Where is it?"

She pointed. "Through that door and then down the hall to your right, but…"

"Let's go," I said and jolted forward.

Emily was right behind me as we ran in our wetsuits. We didn't have to run many steps before realizing it was hot and hard for our skin to breathe inside the neoprene. By the time we reached the door leading to the garage, I was sweating heavily already.

I grabbed the handle, then slammed the door open, holding the gun out. Just in time to see an old Rolls Royce drive off, out of the garage. It was gone so fast I couldn't even get a clean shot, so I decided we'd have to follow them instead and turned to look into the garage where what looked like fifty Rolls Royces were staring back at me.

75

Lyford Cay, Bahamas, October 2018

I found the keys on a wall in the garage. I guess it was our luck that living in a gated community made people less cautious as to where they put their car keys, so we didn't have to search for them. I picked a white seventy-six Silver Shadow and, seconds later, we bumped out of the garage and rushed down the street toward the gate, hardly even noticing that I was actually driving the car of my dreams.

Right now, my focus was Coraline and getting to her alive. There was no way I was letting her out of my sight.

The other Rolls had already left through the gates and, as I drove up to the gates, my heart started racing in my chest. I was worried the guard would stop us and see me, knowing he had just denied me access to the neighborhood a few hours earlier and yet here I was.

I drove close to the entrance, then slowed down, my heart pounding. I spotted the guard inside of his little house. He was watching some game on his TV and didn't even look outside. And, much to my luck, the gate opened on its own when someone was going out of the community. The guard didn't really care much who drove out since it could only be someone he had already let in, so he didn't even look at us as I drove right through the gate without being noticed.

I then roared down the street in the old yet beautiful automobile, pushing it to its limits, holding it steady around the curves, not letting Emily's loud shrieks of terror get to me.

As I floored the accelerator and the Rolls roared to its max speed, I soon spotted the other Rolls—the big red one, a nineteen sixty-five Silver Shadow—a little further down the road.

"Do you think we can catch up to them?" Emily asked, her voice trembling, her hands resting on the dashboard in front of her, her knuckles turning white with effort. Sydney was being quiet in the back seat, but I sensed she was just as scared as Emily. Driving on the other side of the road was still a challenge to me, even in this car that was created for it.

I held my breath as we sped down a curved and narrow street. I dodged a street sign in one of the sharp turns and almost hit an old broken-down wall where there had once been a house before regaining control of the car and getting it back on the small road. After the next turn, we reached a straight road, the town of Nassau rising in front of us, the tires making crisp sounds on the asphalt.

"I do," I said as I took the turn onto the bigger road and the car skidded sideways.

"How?"

"Our model is newer than theirs. They changed the engine and made it bigger."

"Oh."

I looked ahead. There was no traffic at this hour, complicating things. As I pressed the Silver Shadow further, I sensed we were getting closer to them, as I could almost smell the exhaust.

76

Nassau, Bahamas, October 2018

"Get her to shut up."

"Yes, Mama."

The girl was screaming in the back seat, and Dylan tried to cover her mouth. Then, when it didn't work, he slapped her a couple of times. It only made her scream louder. The girl sighed deeply. She was annoyed by this situation. Nothing had gone the way it was supposed to, how it usually went. And now they were running away.

"What do we do with her once we get to the airport?" Dylan asked, his voice shivering in fear. "Why can't we just kill her now?"

"We need her," the girl said. "In case we need to negotiate. They won't touch us as long as we have her. She's an American citizen."

The girl looked briefly at her own reflection in the mirror. The white scarf on her head felt tighter than usual.

Who are you? What have you become?

The girl had become The White Lady after killing the woman who had terrorized her all through her upbringing. She had become her. Taken over her bedroom, taken over her dresses, and taken charge over the people working in the house. Even baby Ella had become hers. She had raised her like she was her own, even though Dylan had grown quite jealous of her affection for the girl over the years. The girl was his sister, and nothing but an infant when her mother was killed, yet he felt no affection for her whatsoever, and as the years went by, he grew to hate her more than anyone. Maybe it was because The White Lady had ended up killing their dad after she had their second child. The girl knew Dylan blamed Ella for the death of his father, even though the girl didn't quite understand why. They had both been outside the master bedroom, listening in, when he had asked for the divorce and said he wanted half of The White Lady's money. They had heard him say that he would go to the police and tell on her if she didn't do as he told her, if she refused to give him what he wanted.

Together, the girl and Dylan had watched through a cracked door as The White Lady dismembered his body in their bedroom and put all the parts in a suitcase that she later dragged downstairs, bumping it on every step, then asked Juan to bury it in the yard. The girl guessed that Dylan needed someone to blame for the loss of his dad, and so it might as well have been Ella. She was an easy target.

The girl and Dylan loved one another, even though they weren't really capable of loving the way you're supposed to. But they shared a love for killing. They were murderers already before they even started killing. Growing up under the murderous rule of the first White Lady, what else could they be expected to become?

In the midst of all the terror, the killing, the burying of bodies, they had found one another, found each other in a twisted form of love, a lust, you might call it. A lust for the kill. And so, they had continued as they grew older. Dylan's mother had been the first of many.

Life after that had been a feast for the girl. She had become the master of the house, and she now made the decisions. The workers began fearing her like they had feared her predecessor, maybe even more. She had total power and total freedom. She could leave whenever she wanted to, and Dylan even taught her to drive a car. Life became luxurious, and she felt like a queen, even though the neighbors still believed she was a servant and she pretended to be one when guests came over, which was rare.

Seven years after getting rid of Dylan's mother, things began to go downhill between them, and Dylan grew tired of the girl. He went into town and got himself drunk one night and met a girl in a bar. Laurie Roberts was her name. He brought her back to the house, and that was where the girl found her the next morning. Sleeping next to him in one of the guesthouses. She stood by her side and watched her as she slept, thinking about The White Lady and then tasted the metallic taste of anger in the back of her mouth again.

So, she beat her up. In a fit of jealousy and anger, the girl threw herself at her and beat her senseless. Waking up from his heavy hangover sleep, Dylan watched her as she beat Laurie to a bloody pulp while feeling strangely aroused. He then left the room and came back with a knife from the kitchen and, together, they cut out the girl's tongue, then watched her bleed to death on the bed, while holding hands across her dying body.

Killing the girl had, in a sick way, brought them back together, back to what they had initially shared.

And so, they had continued.

Three years later, when they sensed they were once again drifting apart, Dylan had been to a party at the neighbor's house, Mr. Sakislov. That was back when they tolerated one another and pretended to be friends, even though Dylan couldn't stand him and his ways. There he had been presented to a girl that the playboy next door had met downtown. The next night, Dylan Chauncey had parked his Rolls downtown near a bar and picked up Annie Turner, wearing a silver wig, pretending to be the pretentious neighbor, hoping he would take the fall if it should come to that.

They had trapped Annie Turner in the panic room and kept her for days. The girl had beaten her up, getting rid of all that rage inside of her, rage against white women, while Dylan had cut out her tongue, and then tattooed her final word on her back, just like they had ended up doing to Laurie and just like they would later do to other girls.

And, of course, the girl had a plan B that came in handy when Sakislov managed to pay his way out of being a suspect. After the third kill, Jill Carrigan, she sacrificed Juan, whom she had grown tired of anyway.

You might say that the girl took over Dylan's mother's position in his life. She wore the white dresses, and she told him what to do, and he started calling her mama. The girl didn't mind; she liked it when he looked at her the same way he had looked at his mama; in awe and fascination along with a good portion of fear.

As she rushed down the road, Coraline Stuart screaming in the back seat, the girl couldn't stop thinking about The White Lady and the way she had looked at her just before she died. The contempt in her eyes. The vibration of her tight upper lip. Vermin, she had called her.

She had no idea how right she was.

The girl glanced at herself in the mirror once again; then she spotted a set of headlights reflected in the mirror, the lights growing closer and closer till they almost lit up the cabin of the car.

77

NASSAU, BAHAMAS, OCTOBER 2018

"You're almost there, Dad. You're almost up on their side!"

I pressed as hard as I could on the accelerator and managed to get the old car up to a whopping hundred and twenty. I couldn't believe this old car could actually go so fast, and soon I passed the taillights and then the back of the car.

"I see her," Sydney yelled. "I saw a hand on the window."

"Was it Coraline's?" I asked.

"I think so," Sydney said. "It looked like she was trying to signal us, let us know she was in there."

"I see it too," Emily said. "But someone keeps pulling her hand away."

"Let me get up on their side," I said, as the car sped up past the driver's window. I honked the horn to make them understand that I wanted them to stop, then raised my gun and placed it in the window. Then I turned my head to look at the driver. The sight that met me made me ease up on the accelerator in surprise.

"Is that…Rosie?" Emily asked just as confused. "The housekeeper?"

I nodded, baffled. The lady that had shown us inside the first time we were in the Chaunceys' house, the lady who had stared at me with her chilling eyes while Emily and Sydney got to know one another? She was The White Lady? I guess I should have known since she was wearing a white dress when I saw her; I could just never have imagined that she would…that she would be…her. I guess it is needless to say that I was quite startled.

"So, one of the slaves became the master, huh?" I said.

"Rather be the hunter than the prey, right?" Emily said as I once again put pressure on the accelerator and the car pushed forward.

Rosie stared at me, then at the gun in my hand, and I rolled down the window to signal for her to stop, that it was over, there was nowhere for them to go.

Yet, she didn't. Of course, she wouldn't give in that easily. Instead, she turned the steering wheel and her car slung to the side, straight into ours, pushing us off the road.

We bumped into a grassy area, ran through a wooden fence, then back up on the road, right behind her again.

I then raised my gun again, and fired a shot at their car, hitting the back. It was a warning shot, to make sure she understood I meant business. Still, she continued like nothing had happened. I tried to get up on her side again, but this time, she wouldn't give me room for it. Every time I tried, she would change lanes and block my way.

"You need to shoot out her tire," Emily said. "That'll slow her down."

"I'm trying to," I said. "But I can't get good aim."

"Here, let me do it," Emily said and reached out her hand like she wanted me to put the gun in it.

I gave her a look. She gave me one back.

"Dad. I can do it."

"No."

"Yes, I can," she said and reached over and grabbed the gun from my hand. "How many times do I have to tell you, I'm nineteen," she yelled, leaned out the window, took aim, and planted a perfect shot straight in the right tire. The car in front of us started to skid sideways, first to the right side, then left as Rosie was trying to regain control, and then it was slowing down, just like Emily had foreseen. Seconds later, we were in front of it, blocking its way and both cars came to a halt.

78

NASSAU, BAHAMAS, OCTOBER 2018

I grabbed the gun from Emily, then got out of the car, holding it up in front of me, pointing it at them, still staying covered behind the car door so it would protect me in case they too were armed.

"Come out," I said. "Hands over your head."

Nothing happened.

"I said, come out, hands over your head!" I repeated, my heart still pounding from the car chase, worrying for what they were doing inside that car. Why weren't they coming out? Didn't they realize it was over?

I heard loud, agitated voices coming from inside of the car and, seconds later, a gunshot went off.

Emily and I exchanged a look right before I stormed to the car and opened the front door. Out fell Rosie, bleeding from her forehead, where a bullet had gone through. She slid to the asphalt, her brown eyes staring into thin air.

I stuck my head inside and found Coraline sitting in the back seat, a terrified expression on her face. Next to her sat Dylan Chauncey, the gun in his hand, placed on his temple, his hand shaking.

"Come any closer, and I'll pull the trigger," he said, sobbing. He stared at Rosie's dead body, sweat springing from his forehead. "She always told us this was our only way out. We couldn't go to jail. People like me disappear in those jails, she said. It was the only thing in life she was truly afraid of. She could face everything else. Seeing her grandparents die. Being locked up for her entire life. Watching the woman she loved like a mother being killed. Being broken and beaten over and over again. Anything. She was the strongest woman I have ever known."

"It's over, Mr. Chauncey," I said and reached out my hand. I shot Coraline a glance and could tell she was about to lose it. "Just hand me the gun, and then we'll talk, okay? I'd like to hear everything about your Rosie. I bet she was very special to you."

"She was the love of my life. I...I..." he said, his hand shaking so badly the gun rattled in his hand.

Coraline whimpered next to him. I wondered if the bullet could kill her too if he fired. If he missed or somehow turned the gun in the last second, then it would.

"It's okay, Mr. Chauncey," I said. "We'll figure it out. No more people need to die today."

"I loved her," he sobbed. "She was everything. She was the only one who understood me."

"I'm sure she was, Mr. Chauncey," I said. "I'm sure she was all kinds of special. I have one of those myself, and I think we should talk about that. About how much you loved her and were willing to do for her. What you had together was quite unique."

"It was. It really was. You'll never understand."

"Then I expect you to explain it to me."

Dylan Chauncey made a groaning sound like he was about to scream, but couldn't get the sound across his lips, then bent slightly forward. I interpreted it that he was about to give me the gun and reached out my hand further, but as he lifted his glance and stared into mine, I knew it was over.

Dylan Chauncey pulled the trigger, and Coraline exploded in an ear-piercing scream.

79

NASSAU, BAHAMAS, OCTOBER 2018

"I'm still not sure I understand this story fully, but I guess a thank you is in order. And maybe an apology."

Commissioner Maycock reached out his hand toward me. We were sitting at the police station in Nassau two days later.

As soon as Mr. Chauncey shot himself, I had called Maycock and told him everything. At first, he had been skeptical and told me he sure didn't enjoy being woken up in the middle of the night for a practical joke, but once I had explained to him that we had Coraline Stuart, alive, he had understood I was being serious.

He had then arrived along with an ambulance and what seemed like his entire crew of officers and I had told him the entire incredible story. Now, as Coraline had been reunited with her mother and we had been able to tell the Elkingtons the truth about their daughter's death, it was time to say goodbye. Emily and I were going home later that same afternoon, and to be frank, we were both quite looking forward to it.

Sofia and Juan had both been released from prison the very next day, and Sofia reunited with her daughter. I had helped them with money to buy tickets to get back to Colombia. The Colombian

Embassy had helped them with temporary passports, urged along by Commissioner Maycock, who I suspected felt like he owed Sofia one. Together, Sydney and Sofia wanted to start a new life back in their home country, a life of freedom.

Sofia had come here when she was just ten years old and was supposed to continue to the U.S. and find her parents and Lisa who had been born while her parents were in Florida, a sister she had never known and never would. But the uncle she had traveled with had ended up taking money from some terrible people and sold her into slavery in the Bahamas, a country she was only meant to pass through on her way to be reunited with her family. Sydney was born in the Bahamas, but there were no records of her existence since she had been born in slavery, in the back house of the Chaunceys' million-dollar mansion.

Once she had been released, and she dared to talk to us, she had explained that she had been too terrified for Sydney's life, so she hadn't dared to say a word when we had visited her. We had also learned that Sofia was actually Emily's aunt and my former partner, Lisa, her sister. That meant that Sydney was her cousin. It also meant that back in Colombia waited more relatives, but Emily wasn't ready to look for any more of them right now, she told me. They were going to stay in touch; that was the plan. Maybe one day Sydney and Sofia would be able to come live with us in Florida. I wanted that for them so badly, especially for Emily's sake, but it was a long process and, until then, we'd have to just call and write.

The workers at the Chaunceys' house had all disappeared. Once the police got to the estate after Rosie and Dylan Chauncey shot themselves, they were no longer on the property. Maycock had explained to me that they had undoubtedly run away and would probably end up in the streets or in the hands of other unscrupulous people who would exploit the fact that they were here illegally. It was the sad reality for many illegal immigrants who came to the islands, he had told me. Meanwhile, they had dogs search the premises and found human remains in the backyard along with Mrs. Chauncey's skeleton in the basement. They were now going to dig up the entire area and try to ID the people buried out there in order to find their next of kin and alert them if possible. It was a massive puzzle and was going to take months if not years to solve.

"Have a safe trip back, and if you ever come back to the Bahamas, then please go do something touristy, will you?"

I shook Maycock's hand, and he escorted me to the door while laughing wholeheartedly. I had to admit, I had grown to like the old commissioner.

"I'll try my best," I said as I took one last glance at the tall Commissioner Maycock, who was holding his belly and chuckling, reminding me for some strange reason suddenly of Santa.

80

Nassau, Bahamas, October 2018

Emily was waiting for me back at the hotel. She was packing up and, as I entered, she stood with her scale between her hands, staring at it.

"Do you realize I haven't weighed myself in at least a week?" she said, not looking up at me as I walked in. "I guess I completely forgot."

I closed the door behind me, then approached her, my heart throbbing in my throat.

"Yeah? Well, so what?" I said, trying to sound all casual about it, pretending like I didn't know this was a huge deal.

She put the scale down on the ground, then stared at it. She put one foot on it and let it lean there for a few seconds.

"I bet I gained at least several pounds," she said. "With all the food I've been eating while we worked on this case."

I shrugged, not telling her she had eaten, yes, but barely anything compared to anyone else. But for her it was a lot, I knew that much.

She looked up, and her eyes met mine. "I don't think I care."

I felt tears in my eyes but held them back. "Really?" I said, my voice becoming uncomfortably shrill.

She nodded and removed her foot from the scale. "I think I'll wait till we get back home."

She grabbed the scale and put it back in her suitcase, then closed it with a smile. I fought not to cry while praying on the inside that she would throw out that stupid scale once we did get back home.

"So…" I said and looked at my watch. "We still have five hours before we leave. What do you want to do? You want to do something touristy?"

She made a face. "Not really."

"Nah, me either. After this vacation we've had, I can't wait to get back home and get to work," I said laughing.

"How about we just relax a little then head for the airport?" she asked.

"Sounds like a plan." I threw myself on the bed and turned on the TV and, seconds later, dozed off, while Emily went on her computer.

About an hour later, I woke up because Emily was shaking my arm. "Dad. Dad. Wake up."

I blinked my eyes, trying to get back to reality. My sleep had been heavy and my dream vivid.

"What's going on?"

"She was strangled to death," she said almost out of breath.

I sat up. "What are you talking about?"

She showed me her computer. "Ella Maria Chauncey. I just read it in the autopsy report. She was strangled to death."

"You hacked…again?" I asked.

"Yes, well actually, it was an article in a newspaper that I just read that mentioned it. They said she was found strangled in her own pool and I couldn't believe it. It doesn't fit. All the others bled to death because their tongues were cut out. They suffocated, but Ella Maria didn't. She had bruises on her neck. And here's another thing: Ella Maria's tongue wasn't cut out until after she was dead. I can't believe we didn't see it before."

I stared at my daughter, suddenly very awake. "And she didn't have a tattoo either. I remember thinking about it, wondering about it, but concluding that it didn't matter. But, of course, it did."

Emily shook her head. "It wasn't the same killer. It was someone else."

"But…who?"

Emily gave me a look. "I think I might know. There's something else you need to see."

81

Nassau, Bahamas, October 2018

I rushed through the lobby, bumping into people, making half-hearted excuses as I continued on my way, Emily coming up right behind me, panting heavily. People were walking, lost in their own thoughts, dragging suitcases behind them as we stormed past them and past the three-man band playing happy music for the arriving passengers.

Some yelled at us for bursting through the lines, and someone in a uniform even tried to stop us until I showed my badge.

"American police. This is an emergency."

I had called Maycock from the car, and he was also on his way but would be minutes behind us. He told me he would call and make sure the plane didn't leave and now I just feared that they might realize we were coming for them and get away.

We found them at the gate. They were sitting by the window, looking out at the planes landing and leaving, looking like any other mother and daughter ready for a new adventure.

Sydney lit up when she saw us. But it only lasted a few seconds before she realized something was wrong.

"J-Jack?" she said and approached us, a confused look in her eyes. "Emily? What's going on?"

Her mother, Sofia, stayed in her seat. Her big eyes rested on us while we spoke to her daughter.

"You were pregnant, weren't you?" I asked, out of breath.

Sydney gave me a strange look. "W-what are you talking about?"

Emily stepped forward. "We read the police report. In December of 2017, you were brought to the hospital because you were bleeding heavily."

"It was so bad they had to bring you in, right?" I asked. "Because the bleeding wouldn't stop. It didn't matter that you were illegal. And then the police came and took a report. You had fallen down the stairs, it said. And lost the baby you were carrying. It said that you refused to say where you lived, and the next day you were suddenly gone."

Sydney blushed. Her eyes flickered back and forth. "I was illegal. I had to get help. I would have died if I didn't go. The White Lady helped me get there. She paid the nurses off not to tell the police, but the doctor reported me. As soon as I was better, she made sure I was taken back before they could arrest me. So what?"

"Who was the father?" I asked. "Of your baby?"

Sydney didn't answer. She stared at her feet.

"I'm guessing it was Mr. Sakislov, am I right? It was something his son Henry said when we visited them. He said that he didn't care if they were black or white. He would sleep with any girl. He was the father, am I right?" I continued.

She nodded soundlessly.

"I'm also guessing that it wasn't a fall," I said. "When you lost the baby."

"Ella Maria pushed you, didn't she?" Emily said.

"Because she knew about you and Mr. Sakislov?" I added. "She was jealous?"

Sydney sniffled. "I…I don't know why though."

Her mother came up behind her. "I do," she said. "Because Sergei had promised to take care of Sydney."

"Mom," Sydney said. "Don't…"

"No, baby. It's okay. The truth needed to come out anyway." Sofia caressed her daughter's face lovingly. "You tried, baby. But it didn't work."

"That's why you helped us, wasn't it?" I asked. "I couldn't figure out why you were so helpful to us when we exposed Mr. Chauncey and Rosie, the people who had let you stay in their house. We were nothing but strangers you had met for only a few hours. You knew what was going on in that panic room. Growing up in that house, you knew everything. You also knew that if we found out about them, then your mother might be released. We might think that they were also responsible for Ella Maria's death. Did you come up with the idea to make it look like the others? To cut out her tongue and place her in the pool?"

Sydney sucked in air, then nodded.

"Your mom killed her in anger for what she had done to you?" Emily said. "For pushing you so you lost the baby?"

Sydney nodded.

"She had a future," Sofia said, tears streaming across her cheeks. "Mr. Sakislov had told her he would take care of her and the baby for the rest of their lives. She was about to get out of that awful place that she had been born into. She could get out of the slavery. The baby was her way out. And then that spoiled brat ruined it."

"So, you killed her?"

Sofia's eyes met mine. "I…I didn't mean to…I wanted to punish her but my rage…so many years of anger toward these people who had kept us as slaves for so long…I lost it."

"And then you told Sydney, and she thought of making it look like the other killings. So, when you signed the confession, you were actually admitting to your guilt. But then we came along, and Sydney saw the possibility of getting you out. You could leave and then start over."

Sofia was crying heavily now, her big eyes staring at me.

"I never meant to hurt anyone. We just wanted a new life. We just wanted to be free."

Behind us, I could hear commotion and, seconds later, Commissioner Maycock—flanked by about fifteen officers in very well-ironed, slightly too big uniforms—approached us. They grabbed Sofia and Sydney, then took them away.

Emily clung onto my neck and hugged me. I held her tiny body close while whispering how sorry I was. I then promised her that one day we would travel to Colombia to find more of her family.

That made her chuckle between sobs.

"I'm not sure I dare to," she said and grabbed my hand in hers as we walked out of the airport toward our rental car.

82

Nassau, Bahamas, October 2018

It was hard to get proper rest when people were chattering and walking by in the hallway with heels clicking loudly on the floor.

Because of the pain she had been in when they brought her in, they had given her something that had knocked her out completely, and it had helped for the past several hours, but now she was wide awake.

Her mother was sleeping in a chair next to her bed and looking at her made Coraline feel so happy. Her dad had arrived as well and was staying in some hotel downtown that he said was the worst he had ever been in, but he said that about all hotels. Both her parents had been there the day before and having them there together had ended in a massive fight, one that finally had the nurses come in and tell them that from now on only one of them at a time could be with the patient since she needed her rest after the ordeal she had been through. The old nurse had given them a good and proper scolding, letting them know that, right now, Coraline needed them to be a united front, united in their love for her and there would be no more fighting.

Coraline chuckled when thinking about the look on her parents' faces when they realized just how childish they had been acting. It was hard to believe those two had once loved one another enough to have a child together.

Coraline chuckled when looking at her mother's wide-open mouth as she sat there in the chair, sleeping with her head bent backward.

She's gonna get a severe neck ache from this.

She contemplated waking her up, but kind of enjoyed the peace and quiet for a little while.

The doctor told her she had been lucky. She was bruised and beaten up, but nothing was broken and there was nothing that wouldn't go away with a little time and care. She was, however, dehydrated, and they were keeping her for observation until her vitals were normal again. And then there was the matter of her mental state. The doctor had told her that once she got back to the U.S., she should see someone, a professional to talk to about what she had been through.

"Can't keep it bottled up," he had added with a big smile that he seemed to carry no matter whether he was telling her something serious or joyful. She could never read his expressions right.

But he was right. She still had nightmares and, even though she knew both of them were dead, she still sometimes felt like she saw them, especially when she dared to go into the hallway to go to the bathroom from time to time and strangers walked past her.

Coraline sighed just as a face peeked in. A frown turned into a smile when she saw who it was.

"Jack! You came!"

Ever since the handsome detective with the soft blond curls had saved her that night in the car, she had been wanting him to visit her. He stepped inside, his daughter right behind him. She was so skinny, her legs looked like those of a skeleton and Coraline wondered if she wasn't well.

"Of course, I came," Jack Ryder said. "We came. To say goodbye. We're leaving late this afternoon."

Coraline sighed, tears springing to her eyes. "Aw. Guess I'll never see you again, then?"

Jack laughed. "If life has taught me anything, it is never to say never."

"Thank you," she said with a deep sigh, her voice quivering slightly. "For saving my life."

He chuckled. "The pleasure was all mine. Or should I say ours. Emily here was the one who knew where to find you. She's the one who solved the case."

"Then, thank you, Emily," Coraline said and reached out her hand toward the girl. Emily took it, and Coraline pulled her into a warm embrace, feeling the bones in her back, then as they pulled apart, she gave her a worried look.

"You'd make a great detective one day."

Emily blushed shyly. "I don't know about that."

A groan emerged from Coraline's mother, and she sat up straight, feeling her neck.

"Ouch."

"Mom? There's someone I want you to meet."

Coraline's mom blinked her eyes, then looked at Jack and Emily. Then her eyes were filled with tears. She rose to her feet and grabbed Jack's hand in hers.

"Thank you. Thank you so much for saving my daughter's life."

"She did a lot of the work herself," Jack said with a wink at Coraline. "She's one brave girl."

EPILOGUE

Cocoa Beach, October 2018

"JAAAACK!"

"DAAAD!"

We had barely found our suitcases before we heard the screams. I turned around and spotted our entire family coming toward us. Shannon was carrying Tyler in her arms, almost dropping her purse that was dangling underneath him, while the twins were following closely along with Betsy Sue and Angela. Even my mom and dad were there, rushing toward us, arms stretched out.

I couldn't stop smiling as the twins raced each other to get to me first, Abigail pulling Austin's shirt to keep him from winning.

"Hey," Austin complained as Abigail made it first.

I chuckled, then grabbed her in my arms, then reached out for him as well and pulled him into a warm embrace, while he mouthed *I hate you* to his sister. Next came Shannon and Tyler, who was squirming in her arms to get down and run to me. She put him down with a deep sigh, hair unruly and no make-up, and he ran toward me, his small arms stretched out.

"Da-a-a-ad-d-y-y-y-y!"

I let go of the twins and grabbed him in my arms, holding him very close to me, smelling him and laughing, realizing in this very moment how much I had missed them all.

Tyler soon grew tired of me and wanted to get down, so I kissed him on the cheek and put him on the floor so that he could roam freely again. Shannon kissed Emily and hugged her, then came to me, while my parents both threw themselves at Emily.

Shannon stood in front of me with a deep sigh and, just then, I noticed she was still wearing her PJs under her long coat that was way too warm for the Florida weather, but long enough to cover up her PJs. Her hair went in all directions, and she had deep black bags under her eyes. It was so far from the famous country star that the rest of the world knew, and I wasn't sure anyone would even recognize her.

I chuckled, then hugged her and kissed her gently, closing my eyes and taking her in.

"How are you?" I asked and caressed her make-up-free face.

"I think…I think I'm still alive," she said, chuckling. "But I'm not sure."

"I promise I'll never do it again," I said.

She chuckled. "Good. 'Cause I don't think our marriage would be able to survive that."

We grabbed our suitcases and walked out to our cars, then drove back to my parents' motel, where my mom had prepared burgers and hotdogs for us that she served on the porch under the huge welcome home sign that the kids had drawn.

I grabbed a burger and sat down, while letting all the chatter and life around me fill me with joy. Even Abigail and Austin's bickering made me happy, at least for a few minutes. By the end of the evening, I knew I was going to be as annoyed with it as I usually was. But for now, I was enjoying it.

Shannon sat next to me with her own burger and had just sunk her teeth into it when Emily walked up to the grill and grabbed a plate between her hands.

I stopped chewing, and everyone stopped talking as she reached out the plate toward my dad.

"I think I'd like a burger, please."

Shannon's eyes grew wide, and my heart thumped in my chest as my dad served her the burger and she sat down, then took a big bite. My mom sent me a smile and winked. I felt a tear in the corner of my eye but wiped it away.

"What happened?" Shannon whispered.

"It wasn't about the food; it was never about food or even about being skinny and meeting some unrealistic ideal she had seen in a magazine. Just like mom told me, it was a lot deeper than that. It was all about her identity and finding out who she is and what she wants to do with her life."

"And she's found that out now?" she asked, baffled, as we watched Emily finish the entire burger like it was nothing.

She had decided to leave the scale in the hotel room when we left for the airport. I think she believed I didn't see her place it in the bathroom right before we left, but I did. And that made me so happy, I could hardly contain it. It also made me believe that she was determined this time around, and I had a feeling she was going to make it. She was going to get better, especially now that she had a goal to reach; she had something she wanted out of her life. A goal that couldn't be achieved if she was underweight.

I nodded, pressing back more tears as they threatened to burst out of me.

"Yes. She wants to be a detective. Just like her old man. Can you believe it? There's gonna be another Detective Ryder in our family. And a darn good one, if I might add."

THE END

ABOUT THE AUTHOR

Willow Rose is a multi-million-copy best-selling Author and an Amazon ALL-star Author of more than 80 novels. Her books are sold all over the world.

She writes Mystery, Thriller, Paranormal, Romance, Suspense, Horror, Supernatural thrillers, and Fantasy.

Willow's books are fast-paced, nail-biting page turners with twists you won't see coming. That's why her fans call her The Queen of Scream.

Several of her books have reached the Kindle top 10 of ALL books in the US, UK, and Canada. She has sold more than three million books all over the world.

Willow lives on Florida's Space Coast with her husband and two daughters. When she is not writing or reading, you will find her surfing and watch the dolphins play in the waves of the Atlantic Ocean.

Tired of too many emails? Text the word: "willowrose" to 31996 to sign up to Willow's VIP text List to get a text alert with news about New Releases, Giveaways, Bargains and Free books from Willow.

facebook.com/willowredrose
twitter.com/madamwillowrose
instagram.com/madamewillowrose

Published by BUOY MEDIA LLC

Cover design by Juan Villar Padron,
https://www.juanjpadron.com

Special thanks to my editor Janell Parque
http://janellparque.blogspot.com/

To be the first to hear about new releases and bargains—from Willow Rose—sign up below to be on the VIP List. (I promise not to share your email with anyone else, and I won't clutter your inbox.)

- Sign up to be on the VIP LIST here :

http://bit.ly/VIP-subscribe

Tired of too many emails? Text the word: "willowrose" to 31996 to sign up to Willow's VIP text List to get a text alert with news about New Releases, Giveaways, Bargains and Free books from Willow.

Follow Willow Rose on BookBub:
https://www.bookbub.com/authors/willow-rose

Connect with Willow online:

- https://www.facebook.com/willowredrose
- www.willow-rose.net
- http://www.goodreads.com/author/show/4804769.Willow_Rose
- https://twitter.com/madamwillowrose
- madamewillowrose@gmail.com

AFTERWORD

Dear Reader,

Thank you for purchasing *Her Final Word* (Jack Ryder #6).

When I was around fifteen years old, I started to starve myself, having the idea that it would make me happier if I lost a few pounds. A few became many and, when I was seventeen, I was admitted to a hospital for the first time, and I spent eight months there. Unfortunately, it didn't stop there and, shortly after I was let out, I went straight back to starving myself again and was admitted once again when I was nineteen for six months.

Now, I know there are many different reasons why young girls do this to themselves. For me, it was about a lot of different things like a tough childhood, but the key to surviving it was finding my identity. I was scared of the future and who I was supposed to be. It was when I found a purpose in life, when I started to write books and then when I met my husband, that things began to change, and I no longer desired to starve myself.

Love changes everything, right? I wanted a life with him, and most of all, I wanted to have children. Today, I am healthy and well and hardly ever think back on that time, but it will never leave me completely. And that's okay. It's a part of me now, part of my story. And, as I was writing the first Jack Ryder books, I knew it had to become a part of his story too. But now I think Emily has found the key to beat her sickness, and I can't wait to see what she will accomplish as a detective later on in life. Maybe she'll even get her own series.

The story of the white lady was inspired by a real story, believe it or not. Sante Kimes was a woman who committed so many crimes I couldn't fit them all in this book, so I focused on her charges of modern-day slavery. She offered young, homeless illegal immigrants housing and employment, then kept them as virtual prisoners by threatening to report them to the authorities if they didn't follow her orders. The details of her life are quite spectacular; if you want to know more, here are a couple of links:

- https://en.wikipedia.org/wiki/Sante_Kimes
- https://www.vanityfair.com/news/2000/03/sante-kimes-mother-murderer-criminal-mastermind

I was fascinated by the ordeal immigrants go through to get to a better place and then what happens to them is sometimes worse than where they came from. And as I started reading about it, I realized it is more common than you think. Here's the story of a woman in Texas who kept illegal immigrants as slaves that you can read about:

- https://www.washingtonpost.com/news/post-nation/wp/2016/08/16/texas-woman-kept-mexican-slaves-for-14-years-said-theyd-go-to-hell-if-they-disobeyed/?noredirect=on&utm_term=.6edc4b0e863d

A lot of the immigrants also end up as sex slaves and being trafficked.

The United Nations Polaris Project, which tracks human trafficking, estimates there are 20.9 million people across the globe that are slaves. Yes, that many. It's a huge problem. As a matter of fact, Jack Ryder's favorite café Juice N Java in Cocoa Beach has joined the fight to help victims of trafficking and started the Freedom Fighter Movement. If you want to support it, just follow this link:

- http://www.juicenjavacafe.com/24716/Page.aspx

Again, I want to thank you for reading this book and for all your support. Don't forget to leave a review if you can.

Take care,

Willow

www.ingramcontent.com/pod-product-compliance
Lightning Source LLC
Chambersburg PA
CBHW030357310726
48979CB00001B/334

* 9 7 8 1 7 3 6 0 7 4 4 8 0 *